The Megaphone

Written By
L. D. Meyer

© 2025 L. D. Meyer
Publisher: BoD · Books on Demand, Östermalmstorg 1,
114 42 Stockholm, Sweden, bod@bod.se
Printer: Libri Plureos GmbH, Friedensallee 273,
22763 Hamburg, Germany

ISBN: 978-91-8080-922-1

Chapter 1

The apartment building at 24 Björkgatan in Falköping wasn't especially well insulated, a fact that dawned on the tenants when Professor Elaine Milton's experiment sent a powerful vibration through the building.

The tremor was a consequence of Elaine's initial testing of her new invention. She had just plugged it into the home's mains and sure enough, the plugs held as she had predicted, but the large antenna-metal box started shaking terribly. The floor vibrated to the extent that Elaine lost her balance. She stood on her head in her well-kept flat, and it took about ten seconds before she regained enough composure to crawl to the power outlet. With a swift motion, she pulled the plug, and the temporary earthquake in the building stopped as suddenly as it had started.

It took no more than ten seconds. In that short time, Elaine's invention managed to cause quite a commotion for the neighbours in the apartment building.

The minor earthquake certainly didn't go unnoticed. So far, Elaine had managed to keep her interest in inventing a secret, meaning no one in the building had the faintest idea what was going on. Outside one of the apartments on the west side of the building, the sunset began to cast its warm light over a well-preserved parquet floor. At this time, it was always teatime for the elderly couple who lived there. Thus, Mr. and Mrs. Eriksson sat there sipping their tea.

Just before the local earthquake began, Mrs. Eriksson got up to answer the phone. In what can only be described as an unusual manoeuvre, she decided to blow-dry her hair while chatting.

"Yes, you wouldn't believe it," said Siw, as the hair-dryer whirred and roared. "Bengtsson insisted on removing the juniper bush. He claimed it had grown so large by now that it covered half the entrance. Yes, that's exactly what he said... What? No, no. Not exactly."

Her husband, Claes-Åke, sighed.

Ulla, who loved a good gossip, could chat with his wife for hours on end. Their peaceful teatime was already off to a rocky start, but Elaine's invention chose that moment to make things even worse. As if that wasn't enough, Claes-Åke managed to spill his entire cup of tea onto the old Persian carpet – inherited from his mother-in-law. The next ten seconds seemed to stretch on forever, with Claes-Åke gripping the armrest like his very survival depended on it, trying to avoid a rather undignified face-first meeting with the floor.

At the exact moment Elaine unplugged her invention, Mrs. Eriksson hung up the phone.

"Can I call you back later?" she asked her friend. "Something's come up that I need to deal with first."

The ever-curious Ulla, never one to miss a juicy detail, reluctantly agreed, but not before adding:

"Yes, of course, Siw. But what exactly *has* happened?"

But Siw had already hung up.

The button on the hair dryer was turned off, and a flush spread across Siw's cheeks as she took a few short steps towards Claes-Åke. Her husband sat in his armchair looking generally bewildered.

"Good heavens!" he exclaimed. "What was that?"

Siw took a few more short steps towards him. Short steps signalled great irritation in her case.

"I'll tell you what it was" she said, her voice cold. "It was you who ruined mom's Persian carpet."

"But dear, didn't you notice the earthquake?" Claes-Åke said, not holding back his astonishment.

"Don't try to make excuses. Oh, how disappointed I am in you. You know how much I love this carpet."

Suddenly, it seemed to dawn on Claes-Åke.

"It was, of course, the hairdryer and the phone call," he burst out. "You didn't notice anything. But it was an earthquake, Siw. I tell you, an earthquake..."

"You always have to exaggerate. I'm tired of you. So tired!"

And thus, the first round of the argument began, but dear readers, we won't linger to listen to such bickering.

Instead, let us pay attention to a few more events in the apartment building this evening.

On the first floor, which was at ground level, lived Amanda and Albert. Not in the same apartment, though. Amanda rented the flat on the right-hand side of the entrance, while Albert took the room on the left-hand side.

Amanda was connecting her new microwave when the shaking in the house began. It was only natural for her to think that the new household appliance was the cause of all the commotion.

"This one's rather powerful" she said to herself, carefully avoiding leaning against the countertop as the ground shook beneath her feet. She hastily unplugged the cord. Unfortunately, it took a few seconds before the particularly local earthquake ceased.

"There, there, calm down..." she said to the microwave, awkwardly patting it before it finally stopped vibrating across the countertop.

"Oh my goodness" Amanda thought. "What have I done?"

In Albert's flat, something quite interesting was happening at the same time. The five members of the band Everrock were gathered there. Normally, the group was a noisy bunch, but now, everyone was completely silent. Albert had built a tall house of cards in front of him on the kitchen table. With a steady hand, he was convinced he could break a Guinness World Record.

And Albert was skilled, no doubt about that. The house of cards had grown tall. Albert's usually steady hand began to tremble. His mouth was clenched shut, and he carefully avoided letting the guitarist's or drummer's mobiles distract him. They were busy documenting the record attempt while Albert's focus was on pulling off the feat. He had already climbed onto the table to reach and was slowly starting to worry if the ceiling height would be sufficient. The friends around the table held their breath. Just a few more cards...

It's hardly necessary to recount what followed, but it will be mentioned nonetheless.

Elaine's invention was bound to cause chaos at that very moment. No modest or gentle soul would dare repeat the colourful curses that flew from the band members' mouths when the card tower fell, as expected—like, well, a house of cards.

In any case, Albert was probably the angriest of the group. After all, he had put most work into the endeavor. Almost as angry was the guitarist Fredrik, who dropped his mobile on the floor, causing the screen to shatter.

During the ten seconds that the tremors lasted, there were two tenants in the staircase. One, a young man named Zacharias, was on his way up the stairs to the second floor. Maja, on the other hand, the elderly lady who lived on the second floor, was on her way down the stairs. She was infamous in the apartment building, and probably in all of Falköping, for her poor hearing. She repeatedly had her TV volume turned up far too high, and Claes-Åke would often complain about it at the tenants' association meetings. It was somewhat easier to raise the issue with Maja in that setting, as she never seemed to notice when visitors called at her door. Siw told her husband that it was because of the old doorbells in the building, but Claes-Åke was sure that Maja heard what she wanted to hear. In any case, it was clear that she had no intention of listening to complaints about the volume of her TV.

Due to her age, Maja was also a bit unsteady on her feet. Because of these circumstances, she noticed the tremors in the building as little as Siw Eriksson in apartment 2A did. The only thing Maja saw, for she did so without difficulty, was 25-year-old Zacharias staggering in the staircase. He staggered to such an extent that he had to grab onto the handrail to avoid falling over.

Maja saw it all quite clearly. Already, she herself had a firm grip on the handrail, and now this young man was standing in her way. There was no other option for Maja but to push him aside with her cane.

Zacharias looked confused as Maja scolded him with a slightly loud tone due to her poor hearing.

"How dare you get in the way of an old woman! Don't you think I have better use for the handrail? And he's drunk too, even though it's only eight o'clock. There's no respect for us elders among the youth nowadays, I tell you. Do you hear that?"

Before Zacharias could respond, Maja huffed off down the stairs.

"What on earth just happened?" he thought. "Was it Maja who caused that tremor?"

We leave Zacharias in the staircase. His ability to draw conclusions was, to say the least, off balance.

And yet, he studies statistics at a high level.

Well, let's leave it for the moment. There is, in fact, one last tenant, at 24 Björkgatan, who needs to be mentioned. The name of this person is Bengt Bengtsson. He rents apartment 3B, which is located on the same floor as Elaine's. Bengt Bengtsson was a middle-aged man in good health. His only vice was biscuits..., and possibly the fact that he was an economist. He sat in his armchair watching the Swedish sing-along program *Allsång på Skansen* when Elaine's invention went off.

The TV screen became completely blurry as it vibrated against the surface, and the sound from the speakers became distorted. "Stokkhlm… bzzz… mm hjere" sounded the signature tune due to Elaine's sabotage. Bengt was thoroughly annoyed. Not because Stockholm became

Stokkhlm. No, he was from Falköping, not Stockholm, after all. However, he had just been about to dip a chocolate bar into his coffee, and now the white sofa wasn't quite so white anymore. Moreover, a voice was heard from the kitchen:

"Abandon ship. Kraa. Jump into the sea. Kraa!"

Bengt quickly got up from the sofa and hurried into the kitchen, where a colourful parrot sat on its perch. Bengt soothingly scratched the bird's head. The parrot was an inheritance from an old friend of Bengt's who had passed away the year before. His friend had been a boat-enthusiastic economist, and Bengt couldn't help but marvel at all the sailing terms Pingo had learned from him.

When Pingo had calmed down, Bengt chose to venture out into the stairwell to see what was going on.

He wasn't alone in doing so. Albert and his four band members came stomping up the stairs, intent on confronting the first person they saw.

"What the hell is going on here?" Albert shouted to Zacharias, with the rest of the band members chiming in. Zacharias leaned once again against the handrail and was about to say something when Claes-Åke stormed down to them, closely followed by Siw. They came in such a hurry that Bengt was almost knocked over.

"Excuse me, Bengt" Siw said as her husband blindly continued down the stairs. "May I ask you, has there really been, what one might call, a local earthquake here just now?"

"That wasn't an earthquake. It was an attack on my sofa and Pingo!" Bengt exclaimed angrily.

"Sofa, Pingo?" Siw asked monotonously.

Bengt muttered something inaudible and joined the rest of the increasingly large crowd on the stairs between the first and second floors. For a long while, nothing was heard but a loud buzz of voices.

At last, Bengt had enough and attempted to restore order by shouting:

"Silence!"

Everyone except Claes-Åke fell silent.

"An earthquake. It's dreadful. There you go, Siw! I'm completely innocent of destroying that carpet you inherited from your mother..."

And so, Claes-Åke fell silent. He looked slightly embarrassed, just as one does after accidentally mentioning their mother-in-law's carpet at the exact moment everyone else has gone completely quiet.

"Now, let's calm down here," said Bengt. "That wasn't an earthquake."

"How do you know that?" wondered Siw. At the same time, thinking that she would like an explanation of what Pingo referred to. It was possible, she realised, that Bengt meant he had been playing table tennis. In any case, it was a funny slip of the tongue.

"I know because I've travelled a lot in my life. I experienced a minor tremor in Italy, and it had no resemblance to this."

"Whatever it is, I think the responsible party should be thrown out the window" said Albert.

We'll forgive him the expression—he was still deeply disappointed not to have made history with his card house construction.

Zacharias cleared his throat timidly.

"It wasn't an earthquake. Statistically, it's very unlikely in this part of the world."

Albert gave him a sour look.

"What was it then, and who is responsible?"

"If we think about it, maybe someone in the house accidentally tripped the fuses or something like that. Is everyone here?" Siw added diplomatically.

"What does it matter? I want to find the culprit" Albert said grimly.

"Yes, but what if it's the one who isn't here who is the culprit" Siw tried to explain.

Bengt stepped into the conversation.

"Exactly! Right, let's see. Albert and his mates are here..."

"Everrock is in the building" guitarist Fredrik said.

"Mm, exactly," Bengt said, distracted. "We have Mr. and Mrs. Eriksson, Zacharias, and me. Maja isn't here. Amanda and Elaine are missing too."

"I ran into Maja on the stairs just as everything started" Zacharias said wearily.

"So, she's innocent" Bengt concluded, thinking it was brilliant news. If they had to face Maja, it would have been bound to fail.

'She doesn't hear a thing,' thought Bengt. 'It was a right nightmare that time I tried to get her to turn the volume down on her TV.'

"That would make the culprit a woman," Albert said.

"Maja's a woman, too," Fredrik, the guitarist, noted.

"At least she's nothing like anyone I've met before," Albert replied.

"Since Amanda's flat is the closest, I suggest we start by knocking on her door," Bengt said firmly, cutting through the chatter of the others.

Amanda opened her door with a guilty expression. Her white fox terrier appeared just behind her, barking irritably at the visitors. Outside the door, nine angry faces could be seen.

"So, it was you who caused this" Bengt said gravely when he saw her expression.

"I'm sorry" Amanda said. "I'm dreadfully inept with technology."

"My precious Persian carpet is ruined" complained Siw Eriksson. "I demand compensation."

"Cookies and birdseed for me as a consolation" said Bengt. "And preferably a new sofa."

"I say Guinness Book of Records…" Albert began.

"My tea ended up on her carpet"

"Stop!"

Everyone turned in surprise to Zacharias. He almost assumed the form of a motionless statue and looked surprisingly stern. When he realised he had suddenly been thrust into the center of attention, he regained his uncertainty and cleared his throat nervously.

"I think you're being too hard on Amanda" he said. "It's only fair that we first ask her how this happened."

Amanda nodded gratefully at Zacharias.

"I plugged in my new microwave, and it just started shaking terribly," Amanda explained.

The others stared at her from the doorway.

"Well, that's not right, is it? Are they seriously making microwaves like that these days?!" exclaimed Albert.

"Of course not" said Bengt. "Zacharias, what do you think? You seem to have an answer for everything, with your statistics and all."

Once again, Zacharias had the opportunity to step forward as the most knowledgeable person in the group.

He gathered his courage and spoke his mind:

"It's highly unlikely that a microwave would cause the significant tremor we just experienced. I'm sure Amanda is innocent."

Amanda looked immensely relieved while her neighbours began to shift uncomfortably.

"Okay" Claes-Åke reluctantly agreed, adding, "then only Elaine remains."

"I'll lead the way" said Bengt, turning to climb the stairs to the third floor.

"I think I'll join you to find out what's happened" Amanda said, addressing Albert, who was closest but, unfortunately, he didn't hear her. He and the rest of the band were already hot on Bengt's heels, heading up the stairs. Zacharias, on the other hand, didn't seem to be in a hurry.

"What a nice dog" he said as Amanda clipped the fox terrier's leash before closing the door behind her.

"Thanks. I thought he might as well come along" she replied. "He probably wants some answers too."

"Quite likely" Zacharias replied politely.

When Zacharias and Amanda arrived on the third floor, they realised they hadn't missed out on much. The door to Elaine's flat was still shut. Albert knocked and called out, his voice carrying through the door:

"Are you there? Elaine!"

Siw turned to Zacharias and said, "Bengt rang the doorbell, but we didn't hear a thing. It must be out of order."

"That sounds like the most plausible explanation," said Zacharias.

"Maybe she's at work or on the train," Claes-Åke suggested when no one answered. "She commutes all the way to Chalmers in Gothenburg."

Suddenly, a booming voice came from Elaine's flat: "Stop that banging, I'm coming!"

A moment later, the door swung open. Albert quickly stepped back, narrowly dodging the doorframe.

The neighbours were about to start voicing their complaints when their gazes fixed on Elaine. She wore a denim overall over a shirt with rolled-up sleeves, and her red-blond hair was tied in a loose knot at the nape of her neck.

Smoke wafted from inside the apartment.

Elaine had smudges of soot on her face and clothes. All the neighbours stared at her, unable to utter a single word.

"Since you insist, I can only say this..." Elaine began. "Welcome!"

For whatever reason, she looked utterly pleased with herself.

Chapter 2

Amanda had some difficulty reading Elaine's expression as the neighbours, in a state of general confusion, stepped into the flat. Elaine clearly had a triumphant look befitting someone who has just achieved something astonishing. Still, Amanda couldn't help but notice that her neighbour seemed a bit irritated. Elaine hurriedly moved a row of paper bags that stood in the hallway so that they could get further into the apartment. Meanwhile, she cast a disapproving glance at them and impatiently waved for them to follow.

"Where on earth does all the smoke come from?" Bengt asked, standing in the hallway. Claes-Åke had taken a bit of cover behind his neighbour's broad back to be safe in case something exploded from inside the flat. Claes-Åke had never really trusted Elaine in 3A. He thought she was generally unsociable and troublesome, and to top it off, she never bothered with the neighbourhood clean-up days. Siw and Claes-Åke, however, always made a point of joining in. Well, maybe not always Siw, but at least Claes-Åke did.

"Did you say smoke?" Elaine asked, looking genuinely surprised. Amanda, trying to be helpful, pointed in the direction the smoke was coming from. Elaine smacked her forehead.

"The cinnamon buns!" she exclaimed, rushing into the kitchen to salvage what she could. Bengt was quick to follow. Albert and his band, however, were of a more suspicious nature. They decided to head into the living room, while Amanda and Zacharias tagged along. The cinnamon buns didn't interest them much. Now it was time to secure evidence and get answers about what had caused the commotion in the apartment building. Claes-Åke remained in the hallway, unsure of which direction to take, but when Siw went into the kitchen, he followed her lead.

"Too late, I'm afraid" Bengt said aloud.

Elaine had taken the cinnamon buns out of the oven. They were covered in a burnt layer and didn't look very appealing. Bengt tapped one of the buns against the kitchen sink. It made a clanking sound.

"Nothing to be done about it" Elaine said disappointedly.

"May I ask you something?" Siw inquired timidly.

"Of course" Elaine replied.

"Why are there smudges of soot on your face?"

"Oh, it's nothing" Elaine said. "It's not even soot, just coffee grounds that I got on my nose when I smelled the coffee in the coffee can."

"I don't quite understand" Siw admitted. "One doesn't smell the coffee in the coffee can, does one?"

"Don't you usually do that?"

"Well, I certainly don't get coffee grounds on my face and clothes because of it" Siw said, looking a bit sourly at Elaine.

"On my clothes? Ah, that must be the black varnish then?"

"What varnish?" Claes-Åke asked, sensing that Elaine was trying to hide something.

"The one I've been using—the black varnish. And I used some red paint too. Funny, isn't it, how I didn't make a mess with that one?"

"I've got a nagging feeling you're keeping something from us," Bengt said to Elaine.

"I fail to see how you could possibly think that," she responded.

The band members, Amanda, Zacharias, and the fox terrier had just entered the living room, which was surprisingly tidy. From what they had seen so far of Elaine's flat, it certainly didn't suggest she was the type to be overly meticulous about cleaning.

"There's something off here," Albert said, walking past Elaine's pillow-covered sofa and its adjacent clear glass coffee table. Zacharias pointed at the paintings on the walls.

"They look expensive," he said thoughtfully. "Like something out of modern art. The colours, though, huh!"

"They seem asymmetrical," Amanda replied with a smile. "But I don't think they actually are."

Zacharias looked puzzled.

"I get it!" Albert exclaimed. "Elaine managed to tidy up everything after the tremor. Before we got here, she readjusted the paintings. I bet she's the culprit!"

"You've got to be kidding me!" Zacharias thought. "How on earth did he figure that out so quickly?"

"We're not betting on anything, Albert," the guitarist Fredrik chimed in. "You still owe Axel for failing with the house of cards."

The drummer and Albert started a heated debate about who was to blame for the card house collapsing. Meanwhile, Zacharias pondered if he could say something thoughtful to make up for his earlier lack of insight regarding the paintings.

"Excuse me," Amanda said gently.

No one listened to her.

"Excuse me!" she repeated. "Has anyone given any thought to what that is?"

She gestured towards a large TV-like object which stood along one wall of the room. It was covered with a white linen cloth. On top of the cloth was a vase with a single rose.

"You know how it is with old people," Albert said. "It looked the same at my grandma's when she was alive. She would always cover the TV with a cloth to make it look more presentable."

"Elaine's only in her forties," Zacharias pointed out.

"The older, the wiser," guitarist Fredrik said.

Albert shrugged his shoulders.

"Okay, okay. I see what you mean."

He walked over to the TV-like object and picked up the vase. As he turned, it landed in Amanda's arms. She looked down at the flower and suddenly appeared a little embarrassed. Just as Albert was about to remove the cloth, Zacharias exclaimed: "Wait! Maybe we should..."

But just then, Albert had already pulled off the cloth, revealing the metal box with an antenna. One side had what looked like a large funnel, painted red. The rest of Elaine's invention was covered in a black-and-red zebra pattern. Amanda felt dizzy just looking at the bright colours.

"Good grief!" Albert shouted with all the vocal resources he had at his disposal. "Come and look at this! Bengt, Claes-Åke!"

Bengt and Claes-Åke hurried into the living room. Siw followed close behind. They were astonished when they saw the source of the latest troubles in the apartment building.

"No wonder the fuses blew," Siw said. "Figuratively speaking, that is" she added.

"What is that?" Claes-Åke asked.

"Maybe some transmitter? It has antennas" Zacharias remarked.

"It also has a funnel" Bengt said. "I have no idea what it is."

Suddenly, everyone became aware that Elaine had entered the living room. She looked exhausted, as if the day had brought more excitement than she'd had in ages.

"It's not a funnel," she said, sounding disappointed. "Can't you see it's a megaphone? I was going to call it *The Megaphone* and here you are saying it's a funnel!"

"What do you need a megaphone for?" Claes-Åke asked.

"Yes, I've been wondering about that too," Elaine replied. "Oh, there's so much left to do. I'm rather tired, so if you don't fancy coffee and burnt cinnamon buns, you might want to head off now."

"Hold on," Bengt said. "If the landlord finds out you're causing earthquakes throughout the building because of that..."

"Mr. Caspar Richardsson is the least of my worries right now," Elaine replied. "Don't worry. I'll sort it out, just like I always do."

She sat down on her pillow-covered sofa, clearly waiting for them to leave. Elaine's neighbours took the hint. After they'd all voiced their complaints—now aimed at the real culprit—Bengt said sternly:

"You must promise us that this won't happen again."

"You have my word" Elaine said with equal seriousness. "I think I know what went wrong."

However little Bengt found that answer reassuring, he chose to leave the apartment and go out into the staircase. Claes-Åke, however, dragged his feet. Finally, he was the only one left in the hallway, tying his shoes.

Elaine got up and went to usher him out into the staircase.

"Just one more question, Elaine" Claes-Åke managed to say before she closed the door on him. "Why on earth do you need a megaphone!?"

Chapter 3

The neighbours left Elaine's flat feeling somewhat deflated. For the Erikssons, the local earthquake had been the most exciting event in years, yet Elaine's muted reaction and vague explanation hadn't given them any clearer idea of what had actually taken place. Bengt withdrew to his own flat, 3B, on the pretext of checking on Pingo's well-being. Just before he left, he said to Claes-Åke:

"Glad we finally agreed on getting rid of that juniper bush by the entrance. I'm planning to cut it down tomorrow."

"Hm… if you say so," said Claes-Åke, resisting the urge to ask when exactly *'we'* had agreed on this. He glanced at Siw, who nodded approvingly at him.

Zacharias took the stairs up to his attic apartment after first saying goodbye to his neighbours. The attic apartment at 24 Björkgatan was surprisingly spacious and modern. The downside was that it had sloping ceilings, which meant Zacharias could only stand upright in the kitchen and hallway.

"Right then, let's head back to ours," Siw said to her husband as they reached the second floor. "We've got a bit of tidying up to do, and you need to drop Mum's carpet off at the dry cleaner's."

"Do I?" he asked.

"Yes, you do. You could do with a bit of useful work tomorrow," Siw replied.

On the first floor, Amanda finally parted ways with the members of Everrock.

"It's a shame, especially with your house of cards and all," she said, immediately feeling like she could've put it better. Albert, however, seemed to take it to heart and replied thoughtfully:

"Oh, it'll be fine. I'm starting to think we need to rethink how we're marketing the band and our music. We haven't had any gigs for a while now."

"I hope it all works out for you," Amanda replied, giving him a quick smile before heading into her flat. The fox terrier trotted behind her, clearly unimpressed by the whole situation.

As night fell over the building on Björkgatan, the events of the day already felt like a distant memory. Life slowly returned to its usual, quiet rhythm. Amanda was just sitting with her cup of tea with honey in her apartment when suddenly the doorbell rang.

"Can I come in!? It's Elaine" sounded a voice from outside. Amanda hurried to the door and opened it. Elaine stepped into the apartment as if she owned the place and casually patted the fox terrier on the head as she passed by.

"I was just about to go to bed" said Amanda. "What's happened?"

She probably sounded a bit alarmed when she uttered those words because Elaine turned around and said:

"Oh, there's nothing to get worked up about. Sorry to bother you this late. I'm catching the train to Stockholm and needed to stop by here before I leave."

Sure enough, Amanda saw that Elaine was carrying a turquoise suitcase. In fact, its vibrant colour made it very noticeable.

"Are you going away?"

"Just for a week" Elaine replied. "I need to get hold of some parts for my invention..., a special type of catalyst among other things. And a powerful transformer, as well as a washer-dryer."

"A washer-dryer?"

"Not for the invention, of course. It's for my clothes."

"Of course" said Amanda.

Elaine poured herself a cup of tea and drank it on the spot.

"Excuse me if I seem absent-minded to you, but I'm a bit strained for the time being" Elaine said. "By the way, what a nice place you have here! I came to give you the key to my flat so you can water the plants while I'm away. I mostly have hydrangeas and some unusual rose plants."

"I'm not particularly green-fingered" said Amanda.

"I'm sure it will be fine. I usually give Siw the task when I'm away, but after everything that's happened today, I thought it would be safer if you had my spare key instead."

"In what way safer?" Amanda asked hesitantly. "You don't know me very well. We've never talked to each other for this long before."

"I know you work on the checkout at the local shop..., but to be honest, I don't trust leaving my key anywhere near Claes-Åke. I'm afraid he'll get the idea to inspect the Megaphone."

"I don't think he's the only one in the building who wants to do that," Amanda said.

"Exactly," said Elaine.

She placed the teacup in the sink and continued:

"That's why I entrust you with this honorary mission. Remember, my flowers need watering once a day."

She handed the key to Amanda and reached for her turquoise suitcase.

"Don't let anyone near my invention," she said firmly as she headed towards the door. "I trust you."

Chapter 4

In 2A, Claes-Åke woke up with a start. A blaring sound resembling the Morning News thundered through the walls from Maja's apartment. Siw was already sitting up in bed beside him.

"It's exactly eight o'clock" she said cheerfully. "Say what you will about Maja, but at least she's punctual. There's no need to invest in a new alarm clock as long as she is our neighbour."

"I'm trying to look on the bright side of this, Claes-Åke" she added as her husband gave her a sour look.

Suddenly, Claes-Åke seemed to remember something important. He quickly stood up and rushed to get his slippers. Siw knew exactly what was going on.

"Bengt is removing the juniper today!" he shouted from the kitchen. "Just a quick breakfast and then maybe I can..."

"Darling," Siw interrupted, her voice sweet but firm. "Let Bengt take care of the juniper. Now, you take the carpet to the dry cleaner, and for the love of all things sacred, don't bother Bengt. He's not your gardening consultant."

"But..." Claes-Åke started.

"Now do as I say. I don't want you arguing with Bengt anymore about that silly juniper. Honestly, if I have to listen to one more debate about whether it's a bush or a tree, I'll lose my mind!"

When Claes-Åke got down to the entrance, Bengt was already equipped with a helmet with visor in front of the juniper. Bengt seemed to be weighing how best to tackle the task of cutting down the bush. Claes-Åke stopped beside him. He carried the Persian carpet in a black bin bag.

"Good morning" Bengt said politely.

"Hello" said Claes-Åke. "You're aware that we'll have a clear view of the road after you've removed the juniper?"

"I'm aware of that" said Bengt. "But better that than a passerby getting hit on the head by a half-rotten branch. If anyone can walk by, that is. This one has grown out over the stone path."

"Yes, but the road nearby is very busy" said Claes-Åke. "Just so you don't regret it later. It's a remarkably fine specimen of a juniper."

"I know" said Bengt. "You've said it before. "

"I won't go on about it," said Claes-Åke. "Honestly, I shouldn't be standing here having a natter! Go ahead and remove the juniper — we've sorted it."

He laughed and dismissed the whole thing as a trifle, then reflected for a moment and said:

"Mind you, if you're keen on a good view of the road and watching the traffic, I suppose it'll be fine."

"Didn't you have anything else to do?" Bengt asked.

"Well, yes…" said Claes-Åke hesitantly before he remembered. "Right as rain you are! I was supposed to go to the dry cleaner. Just wanted to talk to you about the juniper first. But we're in agreement. Oh, yes."

On the third floor of the apartment building, Amanda had just entered Elaine's flat. She anxiously examined the numerous varieties of roses and hydrangeas that her neighbour had on her windowsills.

"Oh my goodness, I'm afraid this isn't going to end well," she murmured.

The fox terrier tilted his head in an attempt to understand what she was saying. Amanda glanced at the Megaphone.

Elaine's zebra-patterned invention remained exactly where they had left it the day before.

Meanwhile, down at the entrance, Bengt was trying to estimate the size of the bush. Suddenly, the massive branches began to swing vigorously. Bengt rounded the juniper and caught sight of Caspar Richardsson, the landlord, who had just inadvertently walked straight into the tangle of needles.

"Ouch, damn it" he said. "What's this!? I thought you would have removed it by now."

Bengt tried to help Caspar out of the juniper bush, but the landlord demonstratively held up his hand to signal that he could get out on his own.

"If you're set on staring at your phone while walking…" Bengt began, clearly irritated. "And no, as you can see, I haven't had time to cut it down yet. But I'm not a tree surgeon. It will take some time."

"Well, it's the cheapest option," said Caspar, brushing off juniper needles from his suit. He always had a bit too much wax in his hair, but Bengt wondered if he hadn't accidentally picked up resin from the juniper now too. He chose not to say anything about it. With Caspar, it was always best to keep things brief. Everything you said tended to be used against you. It wasn't particularly surprising, given that Caspar was a politician and served on the city council. He was accustomed to making his way in the world.

"Won't keep you any longer," said the landlord. "I just came to drop off some letters with information."

'Ah,' thought Bengt. 'Then you're saving on stamps.'

Aloud, he said:

"Certainly. We'll see if the juniper's been removed when you come back out."

"Why wouldn't it be?" Caspar replied impatiently, rounding the bush as he continued up the path to the apartment building.

Caspar happened to encounter Maja already on the first floor. He had just dropped an envelope into Albert's letterbox when Maja descended the stairs and greeted him.

"I'm here to inform about an upcoming rent increase" said Caspar as she paused and stared at him.

"Ugh, it's just as one would expect" said Maja, shaking her head.

"Yes, indeed. Costs are rising. Everything is expensive nowadays, and then we have inflation on top of that. Just to mention what renovation companies charge these days… In a nutshell, the current situation is unsustainable."

"No, indeed!" exclaimed Maja.

"I'm glad you feel that way. At least I've got one tenant on my side. Granted, there's a lot of unemployment these days, and times are tough for everyone. But, in a nutshell, I expect there'll be some protests around here. We'll just have to endure them, won't we?"

"Finally, you get it! That's exactly what I've been saying all along," Maja agreed. "Currently, they call the basement level *'floor 0'* and this is *'floor 1'*. It's a disgrace! We're on the ground floor, so logically, this should be *'floor 0'*. The basement should be called *'floor -1'* since it's below ground. So, a modification of floors, so to speak, would be entirely appropriate. I'm glad someone is finally addressing it."

Caspar didn't have time to come up with a response. In the same moment, it was as if someone had pressed the button to a loudspeaker. A raspy sound filled the entire building, as if an animal were scratching at something.

"WHAT ARE YOU DOING?! NO! LEAVE THE MEGAPHONE ALONE!"

The raspy sound ceased, and the loudspeaker was switched off within a few seconds. Caspar heard the barking of a dog before everything fell silent.

"What the devil was that?" said Caspar, upset.

"A barking dog, I suppose," Maja said.

She shook her head and walked off. Just then, Albert appeared from his flat. For once, he wasn't accompanied by his bandmates.

"Hey Caspar. Don't go anywhere, will you!"

He rushed up the stairs, leaving the landlord behind on the first floor or, as Maja liked to call it, *'floor 0,'* for the sake of complaining.

Chapter 5

There was no denying that Lou, the fox terrier, had become quite spoilt in Amanda's care. He certainly wasn't used to being told off; and all because he had investigated a hostile object in the form of a zebra-patterned monster in Elaine's living room. Considering the courage he had shown in that difficult moment, he certainly deserved a medal—or even better, a tasty bone. Instead, he was instructed to step away from the object in flat 3A. He didn't like that at all, so he decided to sit and sulk while his owner opened a window to get a bit of fresh air.

At that moment, the door swung open and Albert rushed into Elaine's flat. Somewhere in the distance, the sound of Caspar Richardsson's voice could be heard, repeating:

"What the devil was that?"

Albert quickly closed the door behind him.

"Are you out of your mind?" he exclaimed when Amanda came into view. "The landlord's here, and imagine the trouble if he finds out about the Megaphone. What are you even doing here?"

"Elaine asked me to look after her plants. She's gone to Stockholm for the week," Amanda said.

Albert rounded the wall and caught sight of the white fox terrier.

"Ah" he said when the dog looked back at him with

indignation in his eyes. "I get it."

"I think Lou must've accidentally pressed the on button" Amanda said, before adding, "But I turned it off straight away, so I don't think there's any harm done. Anyway, what brings you here?"

"It's brilliant!" Albert exclaimed. "Now I know why it's called the Megaphone."

"Why is that?" Amanda wondered, having missed all the commotion downstairs.

Albert knelt in front of the Megaphone and quickly located the on-off button. Amanda stood behind him, feeling a bit uneasy, her promise to Elaine weighing on her. She always took promises seriously.

"Look here" said Albert, pointing at a black screen that had suddenly come to life on the Megaphone. "It's a GPS map or something of the sort."

He zoomed in on the screen and suddenly realised the marker was right on 24 Björkgatan.

"That's quite interesting," Amanda said at last. "But I'm afraid I'll have to ask you to leave, as I promised Elaine no one would touch her invention."

"It sounds like you've broken that promise more than once."

"Yes, I suppose I have," she admitted, but didn't have time to say more before the letterbox clanged in the hall. Both she and Albert froze as a knock echoed through the door.

"Hello!" came Caspar Richardsson's voice. "Just delivering a letter with some news!"

"He's already done it" Albert said to Amanda in a low voice. "Does he want a trophy for his hard work? Or is he expecting a receipt or something?"

"Elaine, are you there? Hello!"

"We mustn't attract any attention," Amanda whisper-ed. "I'll just open the door and say that Elaine's not at home."

Before Albert could say anything about the plan, Amanda hurried out into the hall and opened the door. This sudden movement aroused the fox terrier's curiosity, and he strolled off after his owner.

In the living room, Albert made sure to hide behind a wall for cover. He heard Amanda speaking to the land-lord. At that moment, he spotted a key on the coffee table nearby. It was the key to Elaine's flat. Just as Albert reached out and grabbed it, a gust of wind slammed the window shut. One of the flowerpots on the windowsill fell to the floor with a loud crash.

"You shouldn't be opening the window like that," Caspar said to Amanda. "Especially not if you're also opening the front door. And as for your dog—do try to keep it under control. I was subjected to rather a lot of barking just now."

Amanda looked a bit puzzled.

"I didn't think he was barking that loudly" she said.

"Oh, he was, I can assure you" came the reply.

The fox terrier let out a low growl in the background. The landlord had a slightly weaselly air about him, and the little dog's hunting instincts stirred.

"I'll bear that in mind," Amanda sighed, adding, "Well, thanks for the letter."

"Make sure you do," Caspar said, eyeing the growling fox terrier with suspicion before saying goodbye and leaving. Amanda simply nodded and closed the door.

"Good job!" said Albert when he returned to the hall.

"I'll go get a dustpan."

Amanda thanked him and watched as he opened the door and slipped out into the corridor outside. She placed the envelope with the informational letter on the hall table and returned to the flowers. Not only had one, a rare rose plant, fallen over, but the window had been left open so long that the leaves of a nearby hydrangea were drooping heavily. Amanda despaired for a moment. Was it beyond saving? No, no. This wasn't starting well. She had already killed two of Elaine's plants. And it was only day one.

As if that wasn't enough, she'd somehow misplaced the apartment key. And wasn't Albert taking his time?

"Have you seen the key?" she asked when he finally returned with a pink dustpan. "I thought I left it on the coffee table, but now it's gone."

"No problem" said Albert. "We'll find it."

He searched around for a while before finding the key on the hall table next to the envelope from the landlord.

"But..." Amanda began, looking puzzled. "Oh, I'm being terribly forgetful today."

"No worries," Albert said quickly. "Anyone can make a mistake."

With that, he went on his way. Amanda was relieved he chose to leave the Megaphone alone. Taking care of Elaine's plants was hard enough, let alone her invention. Amanda glanced down at the broken flowerpot and sighed. Suddenly, she remembered—didn't they have hydrangeas at the local shop where she worked? Lou, the fox terrier, looked at her quizzically as she tossed the pot shards and flower remnants in the bin, then he huffed dramatically and sulked some more.

Chapter 6

Claes-Åke had just arrived at the small dry cleaner's on the corner of Falköping's main square. The carpet was rather heavy, so he stopped for a moment to catch his breath. He then lifted the black bin bag and struggled the final few steps to the shop door. Suddenly, the door swung open and banged into the bag he was holding. Claes-Åke staggered back, forced to drop his precious load to keep from tumbling to the ground. He could hardly believe his eyes when he saw Maja pushing the door open with the aid of her cane.

"Really, be careful" said Claes-Åke, stepping forward to hold the door open for the elderly woman.

There was something about those over 90 that made him speak very formally as soon as he was in their presence. Perhaps it made him feel young by comparison. It was almost hard to believe about Claes-Åke, but he had a streak of humour that sometimes shone through.

"Well, well," he said. "She'd better be careful, Mrs. Jansson, or she'll end up knocking one of her neighbours over."

"Is it him?" Maja asked. "Look out!"

"That's what I said. You nearly sent me flying," Claes-Åke said, enunciating carefully.

Maja burst out laughing, the sound a bit high-pitched.

Claes-Åke chose to enter the shop.

The cobbler, also the owner of the dry cleaner's, was there when he entered. Maja had left her old boots to be resoled. They were on the counter, emitting a sour smell.

The cobbler had already started on another pair of shoes, and a spinning machine was sounding loudly in the shop. Claes-Åke waited briefly at the counter before the cobbler turned off the machine and asked how he could be of assistance.

"I'm here to drop off this carpet for dry cleaning. It's got tea on it... and milk. I usually put milk in my tea, which is fine — unless, of course, you spill the whole cup on a Persian carpet. And that's exactly what happened. By accident, naturally. So, it needs cleaning."

"Alright. Where's the carpet?" was the cobbler's, or the dry cleaner's, response.

"In this black bin bag. It was easier to carry the carpet that way."

"I see, but where's the bin bag?"

Claes-Åke turned around. Didn't he place the bin bag on the counter before? No, it was nowhere to be seen. Then he remembered.

"I bumped into my neighbour on my way in. I wonder if I happened to leave it outside."

Claes-Åke went to retrieve the bin bag just as Albert was walking towards the shop. A little further away, a bin lorry was loading the last bags from a garbage room nearby. The large vehicle's engine was idling.

"Albert, what luck" said Claes-Åke. "Have you seen a black bin bag around here?"

"A bin bag?" repeated Albert. "I'm not sure, yes... there was one, I saw it from a distance, but I think the bin lorry fetched it."

"The bin lorry?!"

Claes-Åke's eyes gleamed with despair as he turned around. At that moment, the bin lorry drove out onto the larger road nearby. Claes-Åke began waving his hands in a rather comical manner and ran a few yards after the truck. Unfortunately, he fell far behind and managed nothing more than looking ridiculous to some onlookers nearby.

"That's unlucky" muttered Albert to himself and then continued into the shop.

The cobbler, also known as the locksmith, wondered how he could assist. Albert placed the key to Elaine's apartment on the counter.

"I want to duplicate this. I need two copies" he said, trying to appear as nonchalant as possible.

"Alright, where does it go to?" asked the shop owner.

Albert assumed it was some standard question that the authority for business ethics, regarding locksmith practices or something similar, had developed. He had already prepared for it during his short walk to the shop.

"It goes to my flat's storeroom. My band and I have a bunch of sound equipment and stuff there in the basement. We need some spare keys in case I'm not home."

"Okay. Is it alright if you have the copies by tomorrow?"

"Sure, but could you cast the mold now? I need to have the key back. I forgot to pick up some things from the storeroom."

"I can do that. Wait here, and I'll be back shortly with your key."

"Great!"

Just then, a disgruntled Claes-Åke walked in through the door. Albert glanced at his neighbour, and at that moment, it was as if he remembered something.

"By the way" he said to the shop owner, "do you happen to have a dustpan I could borrow? It's a bit of an emergency."

"Yes, I have one. You may borrow it if you like."

The cobbler, known as the dry cleaner, or the locksmith, or the dustpan lender, managed to find a pink dustpan from a cupboard. While he was occupied with this, and casting the mold, Claes-Åke grumbled:

"We do have dustpans in one of our storerooms at Björkgatan, you know."

"I'm in a hurry" Albert said curtly.

Claes-Åke wondered what on earth could be so urgent on a Saturday. They waited for a moment by the counter in silence.

"Nice one! Thanks" said Albert.

He accepted the pink dustpan and the key from the shop owner before hurrying out of the shop in the direction of 24 Björkgatan.

In the shop, Claes-Åke explained that the dry cleaning order had to be cancelled. His wife's beloved Persian carpet had ended up in the trash.

"Do you know of any carpet seller?" Claes-Åke asked. "It's been a while since I bought a new carpet, and I think I need expert help."

"In what way?"

"Well, the new one must be identical to the one that just ended up in the bin lorry. My wife must not see any difference."

"Couldn't you just tell her the truth? In these times, it's cheaper than buying a new carpet anyway" suggested the cobbler, also known as the dry cleaner, or the locksmith, or the dustpan lender, or the financial advisor. Perhaps one needs to be resourceful and flexible to succeed as a small business owner nowadays.

Chapter 7

The grocery store where Amanda worked was quiet for the time being, with only a few customers about. She was at the checkout, serving two teenage girls who were buying far more sugary treats than could possibly be good for them. Amanda couldn't help but think of Rebecka, an older colleague, who was always going on about the potential benefits of a future sugar tax.

"I can't help but wonder," she used to say, "why no one's thought of introducing a sugar tax in this country. It'd do wonders for public health!"

Rebecka had a habit of chewing gum while she talked. Amanda thought it was ironic given her stance on a sugar tax but chose to keep quiet about it. While thinking about this, she suddenly felt a pat on her shoulder.

"I'll take it from here" said Rebecka. "You can stock the shelves in the meantime."

Squish, click, pop, it repeatedly sounded as she chewed her strawberry-flavoured Bubba Lubba gum.

"Right," said Amanda. "I thought you were going for lunch now."

"No, not today. I've started the 4:3 diet. You know, eat well for four days and then eat nothing for the following three days."

"Didn't you say you were on that diet where you only eat fruit?"

"I was. I lost five kilos on it, you know, but it didn't give me enough energy. If I'm going to keep up with the gym, I need more protein and calories."

Amanda noticed that Rebecka was chewing her gum with unusual intensity. She'd been in a bad mood all morning, glaring at both Amanda and the customers.

"Just as long as this diet doesn't make you feel unwell" Amanda said kindly.

"Unwell?" Rebecka exclaimed. "Surely, one should feel unwell! The idea of it all isn't to enjoy oneself but to keep in shape. But that's something those who are busy feeling well all the time wouldn't understand..."

Amanda quickly passed her place at the checkout to her colleague. A few steps away, the teenage girls gathered their things, happily chatting about an upcoming movie marathon.

Amanda could hear Rebecka's intense chewing while she walked to the store's shelves. Just then, her mobile phone rang.

Amanda picked up her mobile and answered.

"Hi, Elaine here" came the voice on the other end of the line. "How are my potted plants doing?"

"Great!" Amanda exclaimed instinctively.

She had a habit of blushing as soon as she told a lie, and now she felt her cheeks heat up. It was always very frustrating. Luckily, Elaine couldn't see her.

"Wonderful" said Elaine.

"How are things in Stockholm?" Amanda asked, hoping to avoid any questions about the Megaphone.

"It's as you'd expect, really," Elaine replied. "And I managed to find both the catalyst and the transformer, but it wasn't entirely straightforward."

"Oh, really?"

"However, the most difficult part was finding a washing machine. You can't imagine how many options there are! I always tend to become indecisive when faced with so many choices."

"I see what you mean" said Amanda, waving to Maja who was walking with her rollator between the shelves in the grocery store.

"If it wasn't for obtaining these specific parts for my invention, I wouldn't have come here" Elaine continued. "All these Stockholmers. Have you ever been inside an electronics store and tried to buy a washing machine? It's not exactly done in the blink of an eye. And all these questions: *Do you want a combined washing machine and dryer? What capacity do you need? Do you want a carbon brushless motor? And have you thought about buying a washing machine with Wi-Fi?"*

"Oh dear" said Amanda. Just the thought of being stuck with a shrewd salesman, asking such questions, made her feel uncomfortable. She always felt like they were exposing her ignorance the moment she opened her mouth. Thank goodness for online shopping.

"You know what" said Elaine. "I suddenly felt symptoms of exhaustion and had to step outside to take some deep breaths. Then I came back in and said, '*All I need is to wash and dry my clothes. Any one will do*.' And then I chose the first one I laid my eyes on. By then, another salesman had joined us, and he added that the capacity was likely too much for a single person in the household. Oh, now you're just being cheeky, I thought, and didn't they exchange a glance of mutual understanding about ignorant single women in their forties."

"Oh dear" said Amanda, who also saw Maja at the fruit and vegetable counter and noticed a few drops falling from her nose onto the pile of Granny Smith apples.

Elaine continued her story on the phone:

"That was the last straw! So, I said that a larger capacity means less friction and thus an extended lifetime. Additionally, I added that I could see that the washing machine lacked Wi-Fi, but that was also not a problem as I am happy to install my own Wi-Fi. *I guess you're used to doing the same thing?* I asked. They were rather taken aback and I barely got a coherent answer. *You don't?* I resumed. *I find it quite simple. But then again, I am a professor of physical science at Chalmers with quite a bit of knowledge about integrated circuits.* It really was fascinating to see how much the service improved after that."

At the fruit counter, Maja stood suspiciously eyeing an apple before putting it back again.

"I don't know what to say" said Amanda, feeling a great admiration for her neighbour whose potted plants she had been entrusted with. "I wish I were more like you" she added, almost to herself.

"Nonsense" said Elaine, who had heard every word. "There are already far too many copies in the world. Speaking of copies…, have you heard that Albert and his band (whatever they call themselves) seem to have made it big?"

"What, really?" said Amanda. "How exciting!"

"Exciting isn't the word " said Elaine. "Their annoying hit plays in every shopping mall here. It's at risk of being worn out and outdated within a week. Well…, I'll talk to you later. If nothing else happens, I'll be back by the weekend. Bye for now."

"Goodbye" replied Amanda, then closed her mobile phone case.

Maja gestured towards her and pointed at the display of apples.

"Hi Maja. How can I help you?"

"Ugh" said Maja. "There's a wet stain on that apple. It's disgusting. One could ingest all sorts of bacteria."

"Wait" said Amanda and reached for a paper bag. "I'll throw the apple away for you."

Maja watched as she put the apple in the paper bag. Then she pointed at yet another apple which she judged was contaminated. Amanda obeyed and also disposed of that one in the paper bag.

"Yuck," Maja said. "What a waste of food these days. We never threw anything away when I was young."

Chapter 8

It had been rather busy times lately for the tenants at 24 Björkgatan in Falköping. The landlord, Mr. Richardsson received no complaints about his planned rent increase and noted this with great surprise.

He lounged in his rather grand villa, a mere kilometre from the town hall of Falköping, leisurely flicking through both his emails and the mountain of letters that had accumulated in his letterbox. Caspar waited for a reaction to Saturday's informational letters. His inbox and letterbox were overflowing with all sorts of subjects, yet not a single complaint had come in from 24 Björkgatan. It seemed the tenants were either too polite to complain or simply too baffled to know where to begin.

Caspar took a stroll around the rooms of his villa and contemplated. He went from the large living room, to the dining room, down to the wine cellar, and back up again. He wondered if his tenants were attempting a silent counter-reaction — something like his political party's strategy of avoiding media interviews in sticky situations. Like when MP Hansson, who sat on the board of a privately owned company, made parliamentary decisions that benefitted that very company. Certainly, it didn't look too good when it became public knowledge. And to make matters worse, Hansson had gone all in, posting glowing reviews about the company on multiple stock chat forums. The solution for nearly the entire political party had been not to discuss the matter with the media. To clam up, and thus silence the very problem.

Caspar had received a question from the local newspaper, something along the lines of: *How do you view Hansson's chances of not resigning after this incident?*

It was undoubtedly a very straightforward question, but Caspar had tried to dodge it best he could. *Let's put it this way*, he had replied. *It's not directly in my court. To put it simply, it is what it is. But I would like to talk about our upcoming investments in the local community. We have plans to build an indoor swimming pool for the public, and as you may have heard, the procurement process has now begun. I think this is a fantastic investment in public health here in Falköping...*

And so it continued. Caspar was quite satisfied with his performance at the time. Eventually, the journalist grew tired of his never-ending ramble and didn't ask any more questions about Hansson. That was for the best. But Hansson hadn't been grateful at all. No, he had, in turn, made another foolish statement about not trusting the media. Caspar was thinking the same thing, but he had the presence of mind not to say it out loud. Shortly thereafter, Hansson was removed from his position, and for Caspar, a long-awaited dream of entering parliament suddenly seemed within reach. But the next public election to the *Riksdagen* was still a few years away.

"Hm" thought Richardsson. "What does this actually tell me? Well, it's clear I'll need to keep a watchful eye on my tenants. Honestly, when you think about it, these quiet little counter-reactions are rather powerful. The last thing I want is for things to take an unexpected, and utterly inconvenient, turn."

He continued to wander around the villa and contemplate. Living in a villa hadn't exactly been Caspar's idea. It was his girlfriend who had voted for him to move out of his penthouse (an elegant flat, admittedly, but it wasn't actually that high up. There was a lack of skyscrapers in Falköping). Caspar's girlfriend had been dead set on buying a house in need of "a bit of love," so that's precisely what they did. Caspar was, however, rather proud of the work he'd done on the villa. He'd painted a room here and there, and hammered in a few nails. The rest of the work had been left to various renovation companies. His girlfriend had done her bit, of course—taking endless photos and vlogging at a pace that rivalled the actual renovation. In parallel, the number of followers on her social media platforms and Caspar's self-image as a skilled renovator grew.

So far, so good.

But then the renovation was completed, and Caspar's girlfriend was no longer quite as enthusiastic about the finished result. She kept her spirits up by fluffing a few pillows and changing the interior style from industrial to vintage, but then she stopped. Their one household soon split into two, and Caspar's girlfriend became his ex-girlfriend. It was a tougher blow than he'd admit—even to himself. Perhaps mainly because he felt she'd tricked him into the whole renovation scheme.

As far as he knew, his ex had recently found herself a new partner—an overly-successful real estate agent, no less. She posted constantly on social media, and Caspar couldn't help but notice they'd bought a run-down villa to renovate.

No good deed goes unpunished, Caspar thought, but at least his villa had turned out fit for a magazine cover.

*

Things were pretty hectic at 24 Björkgatan. To say otherwise would've been a total lie—like pretending you didn't eat the last biscuit when you clearly did. Claes-Åke was on the hunt for a carpet identical to the one he had lost to the vicious bin lorry. His wife, in turn, was busy consoling the gossipmonger Ulla, who had accidentally overheard one of her neighbours calling her a gossipmonger. Claes-Åke thought the whole thing ridiculous but welcomed the distraction.

Meanwhile, Bengt was busy cutting down the juniper. On Saturday morning, he had chopped off half of the large bush so that it no longer occupied half of the walkway. That same afternoon, after a hearty cup of coffee, he managed to bring down the other half. Now only the large stump remained, and it seemed to tower over the otherwise green lawn. When Amanda returned home from work on Monday, the stump was still standing there in front of the building.

In the parking lot, on the other side, stood a car she didn't recognize. She walked closer and saw the decal on the side. Falköping News it said. So, the local newspaper was visiting. Then perhaps it was true, what Elaine had said, that Everrock had made it big.

Sure enough. When she entered, the band members were lining up on the staircase, getting ready to be photographed for the magazine cover. With guitars in hand, they were working on getting the perfect shot. The drummer had positioned himself on a step, drumsticks in hand. It was a bit of a compromise, since the drum kit wouldn't fit on the stairs.

Next to the staircase, the journalist was interviewing Zacharias, who apparently would have preferred to continue upstairs but unfortunately was hindered by the band members and the photographer.

"Wasn't it a great surprise for all of you?" asked the reporter with a smile. "Why, to see your neighbours become celebrities in the course of just one day! Rather unusual, don't you think?"

"Yes" said Zacharias, smiling politely. "Fantastic. But technically, it's only Albert who is my neighbour. Not the entire rock band."

"Yes, of course. Did you feel that Everrock was indeed heading for such success?"

"Um..., no, I can't claim that" said Zacharias hesitantly.

"So, it was a surprise. But didn't you notice that they were talented?"

"Hrm..." Zacharias cleared his throat. Amanda saw that he was uncomfortable in the situation and joined him.

"Yes, we did!" she answered with enthusiasm.

The journalist looked relieved and turned to her.

"And what do you think about them planning a great musical tour for the summer?"

Amanda suddenly became self-conscious as the recording microphone was turned towards her. Zacharias tried to take the opportunity to leave, but Amanda grabbed his sleeve and held him back.

"It sounds like a great idea" she managed to say. "I'd love to come. How exciting, isn't it?"

She turned to Zacharias, who nodded reluctantly.

"I wish them the very best" he added with forced gaiety. "Oh, now it looks like they're done with the cover photo. How splendid!"

The journalist turned around and went back talking to the members of Everrock. Amanda let go of Zacharias' sleeve and apologized.

"I'm not used to being interviewed" she said.

"It happened a bit suddenly," Zacharias agreed. "I started overthinking every word I said."

"Impressive, don't you think?"

Albert walked past the photographer and greeted his neighbours. He had his bass guitar strapped over his shoulder.

"Indeed," said Zacharias. "But how did this happen? I thought it was pretty much impossible to make it big overnight."

"It isn't. Not for us, anyway," said Albert, his enthusiasm burning bright. The confidence in his eyes was unmistakable as he added, "We came out of nowhere. It's happened to others before, and now it's our turn. Just like that!"

He snapped his fingers in the air to show just how quickly Everrock had shot to fame. Then he started going on about all the interviews and TV appearances lined up for the band. A minute later, he was back with the journalist. Sensing an opening, Zacharias slipped away up the stairs before anyone could intercept him with additional Everrock-related questions.

Amanda, in turn, had a sudden impulse as she stood watching the commotion in the stairwell. She went to fetch the fox terrier Lou and then ascended the stairs to Elaine's apartment with her newly purchased flowers.

It was quiet in Professor Milton's apartment.

The Megaphone looked the same as before. However, Amanda felt the crackle of cookie crumbs under her socks as she walked into the living room. It was indeed cookie crumbs. In fact, the remnants of chocolate bars if she wasn't mistaken.

Strange.

Just two days ago, on Saturday, she'd cleaned the flat with the pink dustpan. It was still fresh in her mind.

Chapter 9

It was a mild, warm spring day outside the White House in Washington, D.C. A press conference was scheduled for Republican President William Grumpy, set to take place on the immaculately kept lawn in the garden. He was about to introduce his newly appointed Supreme Court judge, Carrie Herring, and do his best not to say anything foolish while doing so.

Easier said than done.

William Grumpy was nowhere near as clumsy or unsympathetic as his predecessor in the Republican Party, but he still had a habit of embarrassing himself in all sorts of situations. The question that most people in the United States were asking was how Grumpy had become president in the first place. Even Grumpy asked himself the same question.

The answer lay in the fact that the election had been between Grumpy, who was 91 years old and distinctly lacking in charisma, and a Democratic candidate who was 90 and remarkably charismatic. Without meaning to criticise their advanced age, the reality was that most voters were not in their nineties and therefore struggled to relate to either of the candidates.

It soon became clear to the public that Grumpy was the complete opposite of the Democratic candidate.

William lacked self-awareness, was selfish, and was strangely power-hungry for someone in his 91st year. As it happened, a popular talk show host joked that choosing between the candidates was incredibly difficult, but of course, he would vote for Grumpy, who had all these flattering qualities. The host's ironic remark spread among the public and quickly became an established expression. One could jokingly shout over the fence to a neighbour, *"In a month it's the election, and I'm voting for goofy Grumpy!"* And the neighbour might respond with a grin, *"Well, lucky for us, he's not the only candidate. But I think you've convinced me. I'm casting my vote for greedy Grumpy!"*

And so it went, from city to countryside and back again. Grumpy picked up all sorts of epithets. *"Old Grumpy"* was a classic, as were *"Grumpy the Grouch"* and *"Gluttonous Grumpy."* In the end, Grumpy was mentioned so frequently in people's daily conversations that he began to be seen as quite popular—and maybe even a little likeable. When the election finally came around, Grumpy emerged as the clear winner, securing a decisive victory. With Grumpy's victory, the public could finally suppress their laughter. Now, they were stuck with him for the next four long years.

William Grumpy wasn't in the habit of preparing his speeches. He simply woke up in the morning, got dressed for the day, and headed out into the fray, come what may. Grumpy often emerged victorious, thanks to his lack of self-awareness, but for those around him, constant losses and setbacks awaited. The President's closest aide and advisor, who also held a seat in Congress, went by the name of Sean Speakalot, and he seized every opportunity to climb the career ladder while navigating Grumpy's every whim. Some might argue that Mr. Sean Speakalot was more to blame than the president himself. Unlike Grumpy, he had self-awareness and a sense of morality—he just chose not to act on either.

The presentation of the new judge seemed to be dragging on. The audience and the press started to grow impatient as neither the president nor Carrie Herring appeared. The sun shone down on the freshly mowed lawn. One could almost picture the gardener crawling around with scissors and measuring tape, carefully evening out the blades of grass.

The invited ladies and gentlemen had dressed in their finest attire and were seated on chairs neatly arranged in front of the speaker's podium. Grumpy couldn't remember half of their names. Where did they all come from?

Perhaps, the audience was under the impression that simply being in the vicinity of an old man elevated to president made one an important figure in society, regardless of how peculiar said president actually was.

Grumpy himself remained seated at his desk inside the White House. In the garden, his guests, the press, and several camera crews awaited, broadcasting live to all corners of the world. The president sat, twisting and turning a Rubik's cube that refused to cooperate with his efforts. His wife, Vanessa, entered the room at that moment, closely followed by Mr. Speakalot.

"I'm not doing it," Grumpy said, not even bothering to look up.

Vanessa gave Sean a look that conveyed an understanding of the difficulty of the challenge he was facing.

"Please, Mr. President" said Sean. "You can't cancel the arrangement and your announcement. I don't mean to be disrespectful, but what's the matter?"

"I don't like Carrie Herring" said the president after a brief moment of silence.

"You don't like her?" said Mr. Speakalot in surprise. "But it was you, Mr. President, who chose her in the first place?"

Vanessa turned to the president's advisor and said softly, "It's because of Mrs. Herring's involvement in the preparations for the press conference."

She lowered her voice, not wanting to upset her husband by recounting Mrs. Herring's audacious actions, and continued:

"She gave instructions for the podium and audience seats to be moved so that the President wouldn't be blinded by the sun."

"Is that all?" thought Sean, but he realised he'd said it aloud too.

"And... she commented on the color of the President's tie. She thought it'd be a nice touch if his tie matched Mrs. Herring's outfit for a more coordinated look," added Vanessa.

"Right, I see" said Sean, scrutinizing the president's increasingly irritated relationship with his Rubik's cube.

He directed the following question to the president himself:

"What can I do to make Mr. President overlook these, completely unforgivable, transgressions by Mrs. Carrie Herring?"

"Nothing" said Grumpy. "I've made up my mind."

"It's going to be tricky to change things now, especially with the announcement right around the corner. But wasn't it just thoughtful of Mrs. Herring to ensure everything runs smoothly?"

"Smoothly?" grunted Grumpy, rising from his chair. "I decide the color of my tie. I decide where the podium goes. And I alone get to decide if I want the sun in my eyes when I speak. Believe me, nobody does it better than me."

"Of course," said Mr. Speakalot, emphasizing every syllable. "I totally agree. You, Mr. President, are the one who makes all the decisions. But what if Mr. President gets the rest of the day off after this press conference, just for appointing Mrs. Herring as our new Supreme Court judge?"

Grumpy seemed to consider the offer.

"It could work. I'm not saying it will, but it could. If I get tomorrow off too, and you clear all the meetings in my calendar, and I have enough time to make it to the golf course..., then we have a deal."

"Heaven help us" thought Sean but managed not to say it aloud. Instead, he said, loudly and clearly, mindful of the president's slight hearing trouble:

"We have a deal."

Chapter 10

There was a knock on the door to Professor Milton's flat, and Amanda went to open it. Outside stood Bengt with a cookie tin under his arm and Pingo on his shoulder.

"Oh" he uttered with some disappointment. "I thought Albert and his friends would be here. I wanted to ask them if I could borrow the Megaphone."

Amanda couldn't believe what she was hearing.

"What are you saying?" she managed to say in pure astonishment. "The Megaphone isn't to be lent to anyone. I promised Elaine that no one would get near her invention."

"Technically speaking" said Bengt, sounding for a moment just like Zacharias, "technically speaking, I wasn't the first to start using it. It was Albert and his gang. I saw them come out of this flat and noticed they hadn't locked the door... but, well. I don't have time to explain it now! That new American president, Grumpy, is about to speak."

Bengt glanced anxiously at his wristwatch.

"Ah, so the Megaphone is perhaps a TV set after all," Amanda said thoughtfully and began to wonder if she had, at some point, forgotten to lock the door to Elaine's flat. She looked at Bengt and added:

"Well, I'm done with watering the plants, so maybe you can take a quick look at that speech..."

Bengt didn't wait for her to finish. He went into the living room with the squawking, happy Pingo on his shoulder.

*

Sean Speakalot breathed a sigh of relief as the president finally stepped out onto the green lawn outside the White House. Grumpy, on the other hand, looked generally discontented as he stepped up to the speaker's podium.

The president scrutinised his audience, waved, and smiled as if it were a great privilege for them to witness him doing so. Then, he assumed a more appropriate seriousness. It should be noted, however, that Grumpy rarely displayed any facial expression, even though some of his devoted followers fooled themselves into claiming otherwise. Nevertheless, Grumpy decided to speak.

"This is a historical day" he said. "I stand before you to announce the new appointed judge for the Supreme Court. For the first time, we will choose a female candidate who possesses all the qualities required for this important position..."

Grumpy went on, listing every possible characteristic of the new judge. In truth, since he couldn't care less about Mrs. Herring, he improvised—perhaps a bit too freely.

"She's really committed to human rights. Especially women's rights, believe me."

Several reporters on scene knew that Carrie Herring could be called many things, but least of all a feminist.

Grumpy went on:

"She takes a real interest in the welfare of her employees."

Herring's secretary subtly shook her head.

"I know from personal experience..." said Grumpy, raising his index finger in the air, thus sparking new interest from the audience.

"Mrs. Herring, folks, she has an incredible eye for detail. The kind of things most people wouldn't even notice—she spots them, trust me."

Speakalot suspected that Grumpy referred to Mrs. Herring's opinions on where the speaker's podium should be placed. He could tell that Grumpy wasn't offering compliments, but rather throwing some serious criticism her way. Sean hoped the journalists present wouldn't pick up on that and jump to the same conclusion.

"Finally, I just wanna add..." said Grumpy.

Mr. Speakalot held his breath, waiting for the next words to come.

"She's a wonderful mother to her children."

All present, except Grumpy, knew that Carrie Herring had no children. However, the audience did not react to the inaccuracy. Everyone knew the president had a habit of mixing up truth and falsehood. At this point, it was like clockwork—no one was surprised.

Grumpy somehow forgot to mention Mrs. Herring's impressive educational background, which made her more than qualified for the job. It was probably a missed opportunity that he didn't mention her prestigious law degree, which had undoubtedly equipped her for the demanding role of a Supreme Court judge.

"Well then," said Grumpy, with a hint of feigned pride. "Let me introduce you to our new Supreme Court judge..."

Mrs. Herring prepared to step forward. The president made a welcoming gesture towards her and proclaimed,

"Theresa Wilson!"

Looking back, Mr. Speakalot was certain he must have imagined the whole thing. After all, no matter how stubborn the president was, there's no way he would have declared the judge favoured by the Democrats as the Republican choice for the position.

Grumpy himself seemed to have lost his composure for a moment there at the podium. It seemed as if he was aware of his declaration but couldn't understand the fact that he himself had declared it.

Mr. Speakalot watched the reporters standing further away taking sudden steps forward, ready to absorb every detail of the scandal. Beside him, Vanessa reached out for Carrie's hand to offer some comfort, but Mrs. Herring rejected the First Lady's hand as if she had been offered some mouldy, wet fish that did not appeal to her. Her nose twitched quickly, something akin to unwanted ticks, yet she and the shocked audience waited for the president to correct his mistake.

"Ahem" uttered Grumpy. "I meant to say..."

"Theresa Wilson!"

The president looked as if a toad, literally, had leaped out of his mouth and landed on the green lawn. Chaos broke out among the crowd. Mrs. Herring's nose twitched while she resolutely turned on her heel and walked away. Her secretary wanted to offer a handkerchief, but she declined the kindness. Mrs. Herring never cried in public and she wasn't about to start now.

"What a total buffoon! He can't even tell Herring from Wilson, and they don't even *sound* alike!" she thought.

"For heaven's sake!" Grumpy exclaimed, throwing his hands up in frustration. "I said... Theresa Wilson!"

Mr. Speakalot hurried to the president and said in a low voice,

"Get off the podium now, Mr. President. It won't get any better by repeating the name. I implore you!"

Grumpy could've sworn he'd said Mrs. Herring's name, but then he heard that annoying voice, sounding just like his own, say,

"Theresa Wilson!"

It was so frustrating, he felt like he might start repeating himself like a parrot just to get his way. At the same time, Mr. Speakalot kept insisting that he should step down, so Grumpy restrained himself at the last moment.

Trying to explain himself, Grumpy started saying he didn't understand what had happened. He wanted to make it clear that he thought it might be sabotage—probably orchestrated by Wilson's people and her associates.

Instead, he said:

"I also want to announce that we're going to kick off the greatest green transition the world has ever seen, folks—nobody's ever seen anything like it! We're going to invest *billions*—that's right, *billions*—to fight the climate crisis!"

Grumpy fell silent, so shocked by his own outburst that he just stood there, mouth agape. Then, something even more surprising happened.

The president suddenly shouted,

"Squawwk!!"

It sounded just as if someone had turned on an old radio. The sound was hoarse, followed by an abrupt laugh that was so out of place, so unlike Grumpy, that it sent a chill down the spines of the audience and the reporters.

Mr. Speakalot stared at the president. Then there was silence which didn't last for more than a second. During that fraction of a second, Speakalot took the initiative and practically pulled Grumpy down from the speaker's podium. Followed by a caravan of assistants, they then, with brisk steps, walked back into the White House. It didn't take long before a flock of lawyers came to their aid. These hurried along the cobblestone path to the president's residence with their briefcases at the ready.

Chapter 11

Amanda suddenly realised she was in a right pickle. Who exactly was to blame for this mess was anyone's guess, although she couldn't help but regret being so overly polite by letting the neighbours into Professor Elaine's flat.

However, she knew it was unreasonable to blame everything on her own actions. It had been impossible to foresee the massive interest in the Megaphone, let alone its surprising user-friendliness. Elaine should have thought of that.

Amanda sighed and gently lifted the fox terrier into her arms. The dog looked attentively at the parrot sitting on Bengt's shoulder. Bengt, in turn, was sitting on a stool in front of the Megaphone and listened intently to President Grumpy's speech being broadcasted from Elaine's invention. He'd brought a headset and plugged it into a socket on the Megaphone.

Just as Amanda looked up, she spotted Maja cruising down the corridor with her rollator. The door to the flat was wide open, and with all the determination of a woman on a mission, Maja steered her way straight into Elaine's hallway. Before Amanda could even blink, the old woman had ploughed over the threshold and into the flat.

"Maja, please" said Amanda. "You've taken a wrong turn! This isn't your place!"

"Huh?" Maja muttered, giving her young neighbour a suspicious look. Amanda repeated herself.

"Of course I know that," Maja replied, looking at Amanda like she'd just said the most ridiculous thing she'd heard in ages.

"What a hideous cupboard. And right in the hallway, of all places! It's just awful."

"Mm" said Amanda, resigned.

"Theresa Wilson!" exclaimed Bengt from the living room.

Maja didn't hear him. She continued into the kitchen, from where Amanda heard her commenting on one of the flowers on the windowsill.

"No, give me plastic flowers any day," she remarked. "What a hassle to water the real ones. I just dust mine off every so often—no fuss, no wilting, and they don't look at me like they're about to die any second."

In the living room, Bengt persisted in bellowing "Theresa Wilson" three more times. Amanda left Maja and returned to observing the events surrounding the Megaphone. There was a brief silence and then Bengt mentioned something about a green transition and billions. Amanda didn't pay much attention to the content. Instead, she was intrigued by how he altered his voice to sound typically American. Yes, almost…

Amanda laughed inwardly. Yes, he really did sound like Grumpy. Perhaps this realization also dawned on the parrot Pingo, who, without warning, let out a loud, prolonged "Squawk!!"

Amanda suddenly observed that Maja was beside her with her rollator. The old lady pointed at the amusing green parrot sitting on Bengt's shoulder and laughed her peculiar laugh. As a result, Bengt quickly unplugged the headset. Maja continued laughing and simultaneously squinted with interest at Pingo. The parrot squinted back indignantly.

Chapter 12

On the road opposite 24 Björkgatan, a silver-grey BMW was driving slowly. Suddenly, it stopped by the roadside, and the owner appeared to have decided to park there. The driver, none other than the landlord Caspar Richardsson, pulled out the latest issue of Falköping News and opened a page at random.

He rarely read the newspaper unless he was featured in it. However, it now provided a good excuse to keep a watchful eye on the square-shaped building across the road. It didn't take a genius to understand that something was amiss, and Caspar had decided to get to the bottom of what was going on.

'It's hard to believe they would have missed such a significant rent increase,' Richardsson reasoned to himself as he sat there. 'Quite unbelievable if they have nothing to say about it. That old couple is always apt to complain, especially the old man.'

It didn't seem to occur to Caspar that the tenants' lack of reaction was to his advantage. Perhaps those who are always ready for a fight end up creating their own battles—whether real or not—just to confirm their perception of reality.

Caspar was dressed in an elegant suit, and his shoes and hairstyle were polished to a shine. He had put on his new sunglasses. They were fashionably rounded and adorned with a faux gold rim. He kept an eye on the entrance to 24 Björkgatan. Occasionally, he returned to the newspaper, as if to signal that he wasn't at all interested in the apartment building. But no one paid any attention to the BMW or its owner. A black cat came walking across the lawn next to the entrance. It jumped up on the tree stump that Bengt still hadn't removed and lay down for a nap.

The afternoon sun shone pleasantly on the cat. Time passed. There was no activity at all at 24 Björkgatan. Life felt so dull that Caspar actually began reading the newspaper.

'Oh?' Caspar thought when he read one of the headlines on the foreign news pages. It was slightly, though only slightly, interesting. That eastern leader Sputtovko had been missing for two days. After the first day, one of his subordinates, or minions as one might call them, had noticed his absence. It was unclear which one. In any case, searches were initiated to try to determine his whereabouts. After much ado, he had been found in a remote corridor of his spacious palace. It turned out he was lost, or perhaps more at a loss than he usually was.

A newspaper in the country reported that Sputtovko was in a really bad state. Obviously, he was as hungry as a wolf and as thirsty as a parched jellyfish. Given the considerable amount of irritation and anger that followed this state, one of the minions quietly admitted that, looking back, it might have been better if Sputtovko had just stayed missing and disappeared altogether.

Sputtovko wasn't exactly pleased with that comment from within his own ranks. Shortly after, the minion who'd made it was nowhere to be found. Then, the newspaper that had covered the story mysteriously vanished as well. But when it came to Sputtovko, it became fairly obvious to everyone that he had, in fact, been located.

In the news pages, there was also an article about President Grumpy and his shortcomings:

"Ever since the President's bizarre speech, there's been a whirlwind of speculation. Republicans are wondering if the whole thing was a staged coup. Could someone have been impersonating President Grumpy? Talk show host Mr. M. Stillwater is on board with those who think the President's nose looked unusually red. And wasn't his hair looking a little too wig-like or toupee-ish, according to Stillwater?

'No way,' retorts a Democratic spokesperson. 'That's just how he looks.'

The debate is expected to rage on until Grumpy reappears on the scene. So far, he's kept a low profile, leading many to believe that it was indeed him who delivered that astonishing speech."

Caspar turned to the national news pages, where he came across a picture of a band from Falköping that had just made it big.

'Everrock, they're called. Hm,' thought Caspar. 'Isn't that something... Looks just like that Albert...'

He paused, recalling the song *Dance* mentioned in the newspaper. Hadn't it been played everywhere by now? He could've sworn he'd heard it in the city council's fika room, at his hairdresser's, and perhaps even on the radio at the annual car inspection centre.

'Well,' Caspar thought, 'that solves the mystery. The whole building's been buzzing with the news and no one's had time for anything else. Of course.'

Just as he folded the newspaper, a small Mini Cooper came driving down the road. It turned into the parking lot by the apartment building. The car door swung open, and Elaine stepped out.

Chapter 13

Caspar had always had a soft spot for Elaine. For that reason, he became filled with enthusiasm when he saw her car pull into the parking lot. He quickly opened his car door and hopped out onto the street. Elaine didn't seem to notice him until he appeared right next to her car. Then she looked up and exclaimed:

"Oh, great! Have you come to deliver my washer-dryer?"

Caspar looked extremely offended.

"Right," Elaine added disappointedly, "I seem to be totally lost in thought today. It's you, Caspar. But I'm waiting for some people to deliver my washer today."

"I almost figured that out" replied Caspar.

"Can you imagine!" Elaine burst out, her voice full of excitement. "I'm finally getting a washer in my flat. The laundry room has been such a nightmare lately! I don't think you can quite understand what it's like trying to share a washer with Maja. And then there's Claes-Åke and Bengt. Bengt's got this almost obsessive thing about saving water, you know?"

Caspar tried to understand. However, coming from a villa background and always having had the luxury of owning a washer, his imagination couldn't quite stretch to such extremes.

"I called the other day," he said, changing the subject. "But you weren't in."

"No" replied Elaine, hoisting her turquoise suitcase out of the car. "I was in Stockholm."

Caspar offered to help with the suitcase.

"I'll take it myself" said Elaine, lifting it into her arms. "One of the wheels broke, you see, so you have to carry it, and it's really heavy."

Caspar looked a bit confused as Elaine trotted across the lawn with the suitcase in her arms. Then suddenly he regained his vitality and followed with quick steps.

"I delivered a letter the other day, informing about a rent increase" he said. "I certainly hope it doesn't cause any inconvenience for you, Elaine. But expenses are on the rise. Life isn't always a picnic, you know."

"Except if you're an ant" clarified Elaine as she began to carry the suitcase up the stairs to the third floor.

Caspar followed closely behind her as they ascended the steep staircase.

"Well, yes," he said, chuckling lightly. "Now, I hope this doesn't cause any hard feelings between us. You know what? How about dinner at a restaurant tonight as a gesture of goodwill? "

Elaine suddenly stopped and turned on the stairs. Caspar didn't react quickly enough and walked straight into her turquoise suitcase, bumping his nose into it.

"Tonight? As compensation for the rent increase?" asked Elaine.

"Yes," said Caspar, rubbing the bridge of his nose, which made him sound like he had a cold coming on.

"Which restaurant? Oh, wait..." Elaine paused, thinking for a moment, then continued, "If it's up to me, let's

go for Tapas, the Spanish restaurant around the corner.
I just love tapas "

"Fine" said Caspar, brightening up. "I'll see you then.
Shall we say seven o'clock?"

"Excellent, excellent," Elaine said, pleased. "Yes, one
must eat. I'll handle it. Trust me."

Caspar was about to ask what she meant by that last
remark when Maja came walking down from the second
floor. She swung her cane as she walked, making Caspar
flinch. Meanwhile, Elaine had already reached the third
floor.

"Can an old woman get a bit of help down the stairs?"
Maja asked, glaring at Caspar.

"Uh, I have a bit of a backache at the moment" said
Caspar.

"Nonsense. Pish-posh. A bit of a backache, he says?
That's nothing! I have sore feet, knees, back, shoulders,
neck, and head. Now *that's* something to complain about,"
Maja retorted.

"I strained myself playing padel," Caspar explained.
"So, I'm afraid we'll both end up tumbling down the
stairs if you lean on me."

"What nonsense! Strained himself playing paddle. In
my younger days, we paddled for our survival when we
were out on the seas fishing. It wasn't something done
for fun, no. And if you got away with a little backache,
you were eternally grateful!"

"Yes, yes," said Caspar impatiently. "I suppose I can
help you, then."

"Help me? You're doing no such thing! I've had more
than enough of you for one day. Ugh... leave an old lady
like me in peace, will you?"

Maja huffed down the stairs, while Caspar rubbed his sore back. It seemed he'd completely forgotten about his backache when he offered to carry Elaine's suitcase. Then, he straightened up and strolled down the stairs with light steps when he recalled tonight's dinner.

The dinner turned out to be quite the departure from what Caspar had in mind. He dressed nicely in a white shirt, slim tie, and suit. To top it off, he arrived at the restaurant at half past six to secure a table. The tapas restaurant was almost devoid of guests, so Caspar didn't need to resort to his backup plan of bribing the waiter to get the best table. Suddenly he felt a tap on his shoulder and turned around. To his astonishment, he found himself face to face with none other than Swedish MP Hansson.

"Well, if it isn't you, Richardsson!" exclaimed Hansson, clapping Caspar heartily on the shoulder, triggering a resurgence of pain in his back.

"Hansson," said Caspar. "What on earth are you doing here? I thought you'd at least stay in Parliament until the next election?"

"Oh, absolutely. But I'm in trouble. Actually, I'm in a jam right now. "

'I didn't think it could get any worse,' thought Caspar irritably. Aloud, he said:

"Oh, sorry to hear that. We'll catch up another time. I've got a prior engagement here now. Let's have a chat later."

"I'll just say this," said Hansson gloomily. "Cannes will be my undoing. I'm finished. In other words, finito, kaput, slut, hyvästi, au revoir!"

"Cannes!" exclaimed Caspar. "You mean that trip with the city council?"

Caspar started to feel uneasy, wondering what might come next.

"Yeah, speaking of restaurants, we used to frequent some top-notch establishments. And we drank a fair bit too."

"Yes, yes. But you had been entrusted with our party's finances."

"Perhaps, but don't pin it all on me, Richardsson!"

"But it was your responsibility!"

"That's debatable," said Hansson, raising a finger in the air. "You all know how I am with numbers, yet you assigned me the responsibility. It was irresponsible of you to heap all the burden on someone as unreliable as myself."

"For crying out loud. I'm about to lose my marbles!" exclaimed Caspar.

"Yes, I know…. Oh, but wait, which ones? I didn't notice any marbles?"

"Seems you haven't got a clue, have you? I'm saying, how can you possibly be so dense?"

"Let's drop the attitude, shall we? We're all in this together, and we need to work together to get through it. It's a team effort. Anyway, I was thinking I quite fancy some tapas. So..."

"What the hell happened with Cannes then?"

"Oh, right."

Hansson cleared his throat nervously.

"It got a bit out of hand. The bills piled up, and I realised we'd exceeded our budget. Initially, I stashed some of the bills away in an envelope. Well, just to avoid seeing them. But then the interest rate started ticking. It just kept ticking and ticking. So…, I made the decision to borrow some small amounts from the city council's budget."

"I think I need to sit down" said Caspar, grabbing the nearest chair.

Hansson also took a seat, prompting the waiter to approach the table.

"May I take your order…"

"NO!" snapped Caspar, and the waiter indignantly left the table while Hansson apologized for his colleague's outburst.

"I haven't got time for this" said Caspar after taking several deep breaths. He tapped the face of his watch and added, "An acquaintance of mine will be here in just ten minutes."

"Plenty of time," said Hansson. "I was just keeping you updated. I'll soon be sitting at a table at the back — you won't even notice me. In fact, I've booked myself on that talk show with Jane, you know, the one from Stockholm. Just to set the record straight when Falköping News drops the scoop."

"Oh, brilliant," said Caspar, throwing his hands up. "So they know about it as well! Honestly, Hansson, this mess is all yours to fix, not mine."

"No!" protested Hansson, adding, "All for one, one for all."

"All for what… a clown, a birdbrain?" Caspar interrupted. "Or, correct me if I'm wrong, but a snob who can't even pay a simple bill? What a daft saying to throw about in your situation! You think it's better to drag everyone down with you? Cheers for that."

Just then, Caspar's evening took a sudden turn for the worse. The glass door swung open, and a cavalcade marched into the sparsely populated restaurant. The waiter became animated. In his eagerness, he began orchestrating a furniture ballet, merging tables with gusto to accommodate the incoming throng. Caspar's attention remained fixed on Hansson, until a familiar voice chimed in from the newly arrived group.

"We've arrived, Caspar! Join us at this table instead" called Elaine.

Hansson quickly withdrew to avoid being recognized as Caspar rose from the table. His gaze wandered from one familiar face to another among the tenants of 24 Björkgatan.

"What the devil..."

Bengt stepped forward and gave him a pat on the back, saying, "Jolly decent of you to invite us to dinner! I had a feeling you had a nice streak after all, when all was said and done. Now, it's true that I'm vegan, so I'll have to see if there's anything I can order. But a glass of alcohol-free wine always goes down well, doesn't it?"

Caspar smiled stiffly, realising that the invitation had apparently extended to Everrock as well. Even Amanda with her tiresome and easily irritated fox terrier had seated herself at the long table.

"This is going to be a hefty bill" said Albert, following Bengt's example of giving Caspar a pat on the back. The strain from the padel had rarely felt more painful than it did now.

"We can play an acoustic version of *Dance* later," added guitarist Fredrik, "as a thank you for dinner."

"Wonderful," Caspar replied sarcastically, and before he knew it, he was wedged between Bengt Bengtsson and Maja in their chairs—like a sardine in a tin.

The former spoke cheerfully about his plans to place an insect hotel at 24 Björkgatan. Meanwhile, Maja had fixated on Caspar's earlier remarks about "padel" or "paddle", as she misunderstood it, and his backache. The old lady chose various types of fish-based tapas and droned on about her upbringing on the West Coast of Sweden. From then on, Caspar would always associate that particular Spanish tapas restaurant with insects and fish.

Chapter 14

Claes-Åke had finally managed to find a carpet that was identical to the one he had previously lost to the jaws of the bin lorry. With a little help from the technically savvy Zacharias, who seemed quite skeptical about the whole venture, Claes-Åke had found an identical carpet on eMarketMania. He then took a taxi to the seller's address and picked up the carpet.

The downside was that the seller had an extra fluffy Coton de Tulear who had scattered a heap of hair across the carpet. Consequently, Claes-Åke must once again head to the dry cleaner's. The cobbler, or the dry cleaner, raised an eyebrow as Claes-Åke entered with the carpet in a bin bag.

"So, you finally found it?" he asked.

"Yes and no," said Claes-Åke. "This isn't the same one, but it's similar."

"Mhm" said the cobbler with moderate interest, peering into the bin bag. He examined a section of the carpet.

"It doesn't seem dirty, but..."

"What you see..." started Claes-Åke. "is fur from a Coton de Tulear."

"What are you talking about? Cotton de what-now? Is it some hair conditioner?"

"No" said Claes-Åke. "I thought it looked more like a small and rather fluffy dog."

"But this is a dry cleaner's," the unfortunate owner explained. "We clean dirty rugs, but getting dog hair out of clean ones is a different story."

"Ah," said Claes-Åke. " Well, I suppose you could just run it through the washer a couple more times, and sooner or later, the dog hair will come off. I'll drop by in a few days to see if it's ready."

"Okay," the cobbler managed to say before Claes-Åke vanished out the door.

"I'm not quite sure how this happened" thought the cobbler, also known as the dry cleaner.

Not fluent in French by any stretch, but a little online sleuthing suggested he was now involved in the fine art of *nettoyage des tapis des poils de Coton de tuléar*. It actually sounded quite fancy in the end.

*

Bengt Bengtsson sat down in his flat, listening to the radio while eating a bizarrely small doughnut. It was important for Bengt to stay in shape, and one mustn't overindulge in sugar. He slurped his coffee. The coffee cup was white, adorned with the grey text "World's Best Brother-in-law" surrounded by an equally grey heart. The newsflash began with a loud ding that nearly made Bengt choke on his doughnut. "*Diplomatic crisis*" it said. "*The authoritarian leader Sputtovko has just been spotted in his private jet en route to Sweden. The Ministry of Foreign Affairs reports that they have received information indicating that he intends to attend the climate summit in Gothenburg. As Sputtovko hasn't been invited, his antics have put the government in a highly awkward position. There is hope, one of our ministers says, that Sputtovko is merely on a general sightseeing tour or has set his sights on a polar expedition to the Arctic and that he, at best, will come into close contact with, hopefully, a rather irritable polar bear."*

Bengt took another loud slurp of his coffee, deep in thought as the radio blared in the background.

'There is so much misery in this world,' Bengt thought, 'And now that braggart is also heading to the climate summit!'

Bengt felt his cheeks grow hotter and hotter the more he dwelled on it.

'No! By Jove, that's the limit! ' he exclaimed to himself, shaking his head in disbelief. Would that windbag, who never allowed anyone else to get a word in edgeways, now be spouting his climate denial nonsense on prime-time telly? Wasn't it enough that Grumpy would show up there too?

'No! Enough is enough! ' thought Bengt and decided to say it aloud too. After he did so, he added to himself, 'It's not exactly hard to sort something like that. No, not at all. I'll take care of it. Then he'll get a taste of his own medicine. Seems only fair.'

Chapter 15

Sputtovko swiftly made his way to Gothenburg for the climate summit, certain that his presence was essential. He believed the event would be nothing without him and had no intention of denying the poor heads of state the chance to witness someone of his stature there.

"They must realise they are nothing compared to me" he declared proudly to one of his minions. They were on board a private jet flying over the Baltic Sea.

"By the way, it will be interesting to see how that business deal turns out" he added. "Is everything sorted?"

The minion nodded.

"We've got the best on the job. With so much money at stake, failure isn't an option."

Sputtovko nodded gravely.

"One more thing" he said, ordering more champagne. "We did bring the Sputtovko game, didn't we?"

The minion nodded and triumphantly brought forth a round game board that looked very much like Solitaire. With that, Sputtovko was occupied for the rest of the flight.

In the cockpit, the captain and first officer were focused on navigation and communicating with air traffic control. The exchange was long-winded and intense. The first officer pulled off his headset in frustration and muttered a curse under his breath. With a sigh, he turned to the captain:

"Unbelievable! Still no landing clearance."

"Damn it!" exclaimed the captain, adding, "You go tell our Great Big leader. You'd think he would have thought about that beforehand. Hypothetically speaking, of course."

"I'll tell him, I guess," said the first officer hesitantly. "Or, if you'd rather, I can take the controls and you can handle it."

"Well, yes, I could. I could, really," said the captain. "But I put a lot of garlic in my lunch sandwich and now I've got absolutely awful breath. So I'd rather you do it, for the sake of all of us."

"I'll take care of it. Right away," said the first officer also known as the second pilot, decisively. "But first, I just need to go to the toilet."

He proceeded to the toilet at a snail's pace.

'He's certainly in no rush' thought the captain as he noted the delay. Eventually, the first officer returned. They were now approaching their destination.

"I'll have to circle the runway" said the captain. "No, that won't do. Our Great Big leader is going to wonder why we're not landing. I'll change course instead. A bit more to the east, perhaps."

He looked irritably at the first officer.

"Well, you were going to tell him. What do you plan to do when we run out of fuel?"

"Couldn't we land anyway? I'd rather deal with an angry air traffic controller than..."

"Than what?" asked the captain, making it sound like a particularly nasty threat.

"...than disappoint the boss. He has a terrible temper. Hypothetically speaking, of course."

"You mean you don't want to disappoint our leader? Or do you mean it's Great Big Sputtovko's own fault if he gets disappointed?"

The first officer swallowed and reached for his water bottle.

"It's hot in here, isn't it? Makes one terribly thirsty."

"Answer the question."

"I mean whatever sounds like I'm toeing the line and have nothing to complain about. But that's just in theory, in reality... I mean, just in theory. Hypothetically speaking, of course."

"Ahaa!" said the captain. "A traitor, you mean."

"No, that's not what I mean at all" protested the first officer.

"We'll deal with this later, after we've landed. Pull yourself together and go tell Great Big Sputtovko we're still waiting for landing clearance!"

"I think *not* landing sounds more appealing," the first officer replied. "I could tell the boss we're embracing the idea of a never-ending flight"

Just then, air traffic control contacted them again, and the first officer quickly put on his headset. He looked up, relief spreading across his face, and said:

"They've changed their minds. We'll be allowed to land, after all, though with new coordinates."

"Well, as long as it's nearby, it'll do just as well," said the captain. "You're in charge of navigation, but I haven't forgotten what you said earlier. You'd do well to remember that."

No wonder the first officer accepted the new coordinates he received. It's extremely dangerous to threaten someone you directly depend on. For the reader's information, it can be mentioned that threats against dentists, car inspectors, opticians, estate agents, candy shop owners, kitchen staff, hairdressers, ticket inspectors, and nearby discus-throwing clubs, always tend to backfire.

Or, hold on a moment... threats in any direction tend to backfire. Like a boomerang, they always come right back at you. Therefore, it wasn't the first officer's fault that Sputtovko's private jet went astray. No, the captain had already set the ball rolling. Or rather the private jet. And perhaps, in a small way, a certain Bengt Bengtsson in Falköping was also to blame for the upcoming events.

*

Grumpy had his sights set on the climate summit in Gothenburg as well. Truth be told, he had little desire to attend the summit. It was Mr. Speakalot who had conveyed the benefits of participating, and he had succeeded in this seemingly hopeless endeavor.

Grumpy would once again have the opportunity to grace the world stage and capture everyone's attention. It was as good a reason as any, thought Grumpy, as he willingly boarded his presidential aircraft to Gothenburg. The journey proved more successful than that of Sputtovko's private jet, but then again, for once, Grumpy had the good sense not to threaten anyone—especially not one of the pilots. He might have made a threat to Mr. Speakalot, though, but the latter simply faced his bad temper with an unshaken countenance. Grumpy was tempted to annoy his subordinate further, aiming to provoke some sort of reaction. He took a deep breath and then hinted that the mishap during the appointment of the new judge could potentially recur at the climate summit.

"I'm probably gonna say something stupid again," he exclaimed. "But you were absolutely sure, Speakalot, right? You said it wouldn't happen again because there was something wrong with the microphone."

"Hrm," began Mr. Speakalot. "The Secret Service did suggest it was sabotage. I just said that there might have been something wrong with the microphone."

"And you all seem pretty sure it won't happen again, right? Let me warn you, if anything else happens, you're all fired."

"Sorry," said Mr. Speakalot. "What sort of potential mess-up are we discussing?"

Disaster! He had said it aloud.

"I apologize, Mr. President. I believe I nodded off for a second."

"We don't nod off here!" uttered the president grumpily. "Nod off. That's the worst I've ever heard."

Mr. Speakalot exhaled. Grumpy had reacted to the latter and not noticed his previous comment. A few minutes later, Mr. Speakalot got a moment's break from his boss. The president had nodded off in his comfy seat and was snoring loudly.

Grumpy was not at all prepared to make any significant concessions at the climate summit. Surely Mother Earth would have thanked him if he had stayed at home considering the emissions of his private jet. But Grumpy didn't like to listen to Mother Earth and thus didn't heed her advice. Nature wasn't Grumpy's jam. No, he was more of a concrete enthusiast. In his world, if there was a problem, one could count on him to fix it with bricks and mortar. Housing crisis? Build more houses. Traffic jam? Build more roads. Unemployment? Build more offices. Inflation? Build more stores. And as for climate change, well, Grumpy didn't contemplate wind turbines and solar panels. His solution was to keep expanding his business empire. Because in his mind, more dollars equalled less crisis. Since more money would result in him getting richer, and because wealth (according to Grumpy) solves all sorts of predicaments, it would probably also prove effective against a climate crisis. And what if there really was climate change on the horizon? Well, Grumpy certainly wasn't buying it.

Chapter 16

Elaine was beginning to suspect that something was amiss with the Megaphone. There were certain indications that someone had been tampering with it. On that same day, when she returned home from the grocer's, she discovered that the door to her flat was left unlocked.

"Hold your horses!" a voice was heard from inside the flat. "If you really want to use the Megaphone, you must wait in line."

She opened the door to the flat and stepped in, her pulse pounding in her temples.

'How dare they enter uninvited!' she thought, as she rounded the hallway into the living room. There, gathered together, were all the members of Everrock, along with Bengt Bengtsson.

Not according to standard, Pingo had been left behind in Bengt's flat following the parrot's 'feather-in-mouth' moment during Grumpy's speech.

"WHAT in the world is this!?" Elaine roared with unexpected vocal strength.

The murmur among the band members died down, and Bengt's instructions for the queue finally came to an end.

"Unbelievable! I go out for an hour of shopping," Elaine continued, "and when I come back, my home's under siege!"

Bengt looked uncharacteristically timid as he said,

"It's quite a remarkable invention. Ahem, Megaphone that you've got here, Elaine."

"I have never experienced anything like this!" Elaine proclaimed.

Her red-blonde hair was uncombed and fell over her shoulders like flames. At that moment, she strongly resembled an angry lioness about to attack.

"Well, Everrock," Bengt said with a sigh, "I suppose we'd better apologize and let Elaine have some peace and quiet."

"Sorry," Axel, the drummer, said, standing closest.

The rest of the band quickly followed suit, lining up in what looked like a proper queue.

"We just wanted to launch our latest song, *Swing*," Albert explained, once the others had left for the stairwell.

"Do I look remotely interested?" Elaine asked rhetorically.

Albert looked as though he'd just been deeply insulted and muttered an apology before retreating towards the hall. Then it was Bengt's turn.

"My apologies, Elaine," he said. "I assumed you were at work. But think about this: The Megaphone is a remarkable invention. You've helped President Grumpy announce..."

"Do I look remotely interested?" Elaine interjected coldly.

"But surely you are? Who wouldn't be?"

"I have no opinion on the matter," Elaine retorted. "And don't you think there will be consequences of your actions? The Megaphone wasn't intended for this sort of nonsense."

"Nonsense!"

This time, it was Bengt who looked deeply offended.

"How can you dismiss it as nonsense when the fate of the world's climate hangs in the balance? And what was the Megaphone truly meant for if not to change the world?"

"It's a play on words," Elaine said, clearly impatient. "The Megaphone was meant for its opposite."

Bengt seemed to ponder this, but Elaine gave him no time for reflection.

"All I wanted was a bit of peace and quiet," she stated. "I wanted some silence! But the Megaphone lives up to its name, in a way. Right now, it's just **chaos and noise— disorder and constant arguments**"

She stared intently at Bengt Bengtsson, who took the hint and again apologized before leaving the flat.

Elaine slammed the door behind her uninvited guests. Afterwards, she paused in the hall for a moment. She exhaled slowly and tried to calm down. Then she went into the living room and looked at her zebra-patterned invention.

"I need to get you sorted. Oh, I really do feel stressed out. If only I could get some peace and quiet."

She glared at the Megaphone and then clenched her fist in its direction.

"What havoc you've wrought! I was hoping for peace, but instead, I'm more wound up than ever."

After Professor Elaine had vented her frustration at the Megaphone, she settled onto her broad sofa and took several deep breaths. She had learned from the TV show *Trust Me, I'm a Psychiatrist* that this could help soothe frayed nerves in tense situations. Actually, it was really relaxing. To the extent that Elaine fell asleep.

When she opened her eyes again, the darkness had settled over Falköping. Perched on a branch of the poplar tree outside her rectangular window (windows usually take that shape), a blackbird sang its heart out. Elaine sat in her spacious sofa, gazing at the poplar and the blackbird.

Feeling somewhat composed now, she began to mull over a few things. For instance, had she ever laid eyes on a triangular window?

'One encounters circular windows,' she reasoned. 'But never triangular ones. I wonder why? What if I experimented with fitting a triangular window? I could patent it and become wealthy. Wealthy enough to relocate to some remote island where people would let me be. It might be easier than fixing the Megaphone.'

The notion had promise until she considered the landlord.

'There's probably a limit to what Caspar would allow. I wouldn't get his consent to install a triangular window in my flat.' As Elaine distanced herself from her idea in this manner, she began to see its absurdity.

'I can't even sit down and listen to a little blackbird singing on a poplar branch without work creeping into my thoughts. It's quite dire.'

With that, she shed a few metaphorical tears. Crying had never come easily to Elaine, but she had mastered the art of sobbing without shedding tears. And that was precisely the art she practised in that moment.

Chapter 17

The mist hung like creamy custard around Sputtovko's private jet. He sat gazing out of the window without truly seeing anything at all. This was rather typical for the leader, though he usually didn't have the elements to contend with.

"Misty," he remarked. One seat away, a minion agreed with a nod. Sputtovko could have just as easily claimed that the weather was remarkably fine and still received a nod of agreement. It was, therefore, a perfect setup for *fake news*. Given the questionable accuracy of weather forecasts, the weather could have turned out to be just about anything, but unfortunately for Sputtovko, it really was foggy. In any case, he never referred to *fake news* by that name. In his world, they were rather called "Sputtovko's truths" and all other kinds of news were malicious and aimed to irritate him personally. This was just one example of how complicated his existence was. Not to mention that Sputtovko's grip as an authoritarian leader depended on the whims and fancies of another authoritarian leader. But his situation was about to become even more tangled when his jet finally touched down.

When the stairs had been rolled out and all the passengers had disembarked from the plane, they stood on the tarmac and surveyed their surroundings. A man in a hi-vis vest stood further away, gawping at the group without making any attempt to approach them.

"Where's the welcoming committee?" Sputtovko asked, disillusioned. The minions stood silent and solemn.

"I don't think there'll be a welcoming committee," said the captain, who was just descending the stairs of the plane.

"I'll leave it to him to explain further," he continued, turning around to await the first officer's arrival. His colleague then joined the small group on the ground, stumbling on unsteady legs.

The hi-vis-clad man further away continued to stare at them.

"Well?" Sputtovko demanded, his voice laced with steel as he fixed his gaze on the second pilot. But before any further words could be exchanged, the latter abruptly spun on his heel and dashed off into the mist at the pace of a champion sprinter. The captain let out a frustrated cry, his disbelief obvious at his colleague's sudden departure.

"Get him!" he instructed Sputtovko's bodyguards, declaring that they were dealing with a traitor. Two of the guards disappeared into the mist in pursuit of the second pilot. And just like that, Sputtovko's entourage was three members short.

"A traitor indeed," declared Sputtovko, grilling the captain thoroughly to unearth the circumstances. When the interrogation concluded, he surveyed the scene and exclaimed:

"What sort of person is staring so at Sputtovko!?"

"A complete nobody, obviously," remarked one of the minions, and Sputtovko felt his calm return. "He's likely never encountered a leader of your calibre before."

"Sounds about right," said Sputtovko, letting out a hearty laugh. Then he fell silent abruptly. The unpleasant character in the high-vis vest had raised a white, round sign, mounted on a stick, into the air. The man continued to stare at Sputtovko's entourage as if he were utterly shocked to find them there.

"What's the meaning of this?" exclaimed the leader irritably. "Make sure someone tells that individual that Sputtovko disapproves of his attitude and placard stick. Right now! Immediately!"

An English-speaking minion hurried off and engaged in a verbose conversation with the man. He received a terse response.

"What did he say?" asked the leader when the interpreter returned.

"He says we should move on right away, if I understood correctly."

"Right away?! Who does this impudent individual think he is? Where Sputtovko has landed, there he stays. Understood!"

And with that, he hurled a few choice swear words at the man in question.

At that moment, a loud bang was heard.

All members of the party turned to see the jet swaying for a fraction of a second. Then the front landing gear collapsed, and the nose of the plane plummeted towards the ground with all its weight. The captain was relieved to have left the cockpit when its window shattered into a thousand pieces.

Now it was Sputtovko's turn to gawp. He surveyed the wreckage of his luxurious jet without uttering a single word.

Slowly emerging from the mist was a steamroller with a driver.

"Good grief!" exclaimed the driver. "Who on earth thought it was a good idea to park an airplane on a freshly laid runway?"

Sputtovko was about to step aside to confer with his entourage when he realised he couldn't budge an inch. He peered down at his shoes, which had sunk into the warm asphalt.

The ongoing sequence of events presented a rather strange spectacle in every respect. Those who hadn't become ensnared in the macadam were forced to fetch planks to assist in the rescue operation. Sputtovko puffed on his moustache as he endeavoured to maintain his balance. They had to begin by lifting him out of his shoes and then transferring him to safer ground.

"I never ever wish to see that individual again!" exclaimed Sputtovko and gestured to the hi-vis-clad man, so taken aback that he forgot to refer to himself in the third person. The English-speaking minion, on the other hand, inquired why Sputtovko received such a strange reception. Did all residents of Gothenburg behave in such a manner, he wished to ascertain.

"Residents of Gothenburg?" echoed the hi-vis-clad man, whose real name was Peter, and continued:

"There are no residents of Gothenburg here."

"Most peculiar," remarked the interpreter. "Are you implying that we are not in Gothenburg?"

"Well, one can certainly get lost in the fog, but you are, quite extremely, off course. You're on Åland," said Peter.

"What kind of place is Åland?" wondered the interpreter, lacking geographical knowledge in that respect.

"It's an island," Peter replied curtly. "May I ask who that moustachioed fellow is? Seems to think quite highly of himself, doesn't he?"

"Er, yes," began the interpreter. "An island indeed. And this island belongs to Sweden then?"

"No, goodness no. We're actually further east, towards Finland. Although we're not far from the Swedish east coast, really. Anyway, there's going to be a lot of paperwork after this airplane incident. The bureaucracy will be in full swing," Peter said.

"So, we're in Finland then?" asked the interpreter, scratching his head. "Do you speak Finnish?"

"Don't you realise we're speaking English?" uttered Peter, starting to get a bit irritated with the interpreter. "Normally, I speak Swedish. Not Finnish. And we're not in Finland at all. We're on Åland, which belongs to Finland but is self-governing."

"Oh," exclaimed the interpreter nervously, clasping his hands. "But what should I convey to Honourable Sputtovko?"

"Is he the one with the moustache? Ugh, so it's him then. More dishonourable than honourable he is, if you ask me. Why would he choose to land at my workplace of all places?" Peter grumbled.

Suddenly, it seemed like the interpreter had come up with a new approach to locating themselves.

"So, you're Swedish since you speak Swedish?" he asked.

"I'm Finnish," the driver of the steamroller sharply interjected.

"Me too," agreed Peter. "But let's put aside all this talk of nationalities. It's just silly. At the moment, the priority is to sort out the paperwork."

The interpreter returned crestfallen to his superior, attempting to explain where they had ended up.

Sputtovko was not pleased, but then again, he stood there in his socks, feeling the chill nibbling at his toes.

Chapter 18

At 24 Björkgatan in Falköping, a temporary sense of peace had settled. Claes-Åke had returned the Persian carpet to its rightful place in the home. He then made sure Elaine wasn't planning to activate the Megaphone by knocking on her door and asking directly. Elaine assured him that she had no intention of starting up the machine again but instead planned to rebuild it. That answer had to suffice for Claes-Åke, who felt reassured enough to enjoy his evening tea in the armchair beside the Persian carpet.

His wife was particularly delighted with the results of the dry cleaning and launched into a lengthy monologue. She could hardly believe her eyes when she saw the transformation. Not only was the carpet free of the tea stain, but it also looked as good as new. Its lustre had been restored, the previously worn and frayed fringes were now in perfect condition, and the pile, which had grown a few centimetres, appeared noticeably fuller throughout.

Claes-Åke didn't appreciate her thorough inspection of the carpet. He feared that some small detail might betray him at any moment. Heaven help him if she discovered the secret! Heirlooms like this, passed down through generations, meant a great deal to Siw. Claes-Åke was determined to preserve the peace. In his mind, he had even come up with a little poem on the matter. It went something like this:

> *"Tread lightly, preserve the peace of our home,*
> *Let it endure,*
> *In the sunlight of tomorrow's waters,*
> *On the waves of blue.*
>
> *Speak softly, preserve the peace of our home,*
> *Amid all the things we may possess,*
> *With evening's glow through the summer night,*
> *I long only to reach the peace of our home."*

Claes-Åke was quite pleased with his poem. He took pride in being a bit of a poet and wordsmith on the side. He had written the poem on the back of a cereal box, but unfortunately, Siw had accidentally thrown the package away when the cereal ran out. Claes-Åke had even written a poem about that, too. In a way, it felt quite poetic—this little piece of poetry ending up in the bin. Now, he had started to keep his poems in his memory instead. It felt safer and was good mental exercise as he got older. And as a retiree, you always had to have something to occupy your time.

*

The juniper had been cut down some time ago. No one would have to get tangled in its bushy branches on their way to the entrance of the building anymore, and Caspar Richardsson was spared from getting resin in his hair, which could have been mistaken for an overzealous application of hair wax.

All was well and good, except for the juniper stump, which stood in all its glory beside the gravel path.

"Time to dig out the stump, don't you think?" Claes-Åke remarked to Bengt when they crossed paths in the laundry room. Claes-Åke prided himself on his readiness to help. Noticing Bengt's puzzled expression, Claes-Åke immediately began offering various ideas on how they might tackle the stubborn tree stump.

"I suggest," said Claes-Åke, "we use a larger car with a tow hitch, attach a rope, and then, easy as pie, just pull the stump away."

Bengt peered into the spinning washing machine. He had set it to Eco-mode, which annoyed Claes-Åke no end. Eco-mode took four hours, far longer than the usual laundry time. For some reason, Claes-Åke always seemed to end up behind Bengt in the schedule, despite his best efforts to avoid it.

"At nine o'clock on a Sunday morning," he would think to himself, "That's when I'll get ahead. Bengt will want to sleep in and won't have time to take the slot before me."

But no, Bengt always turned up at the last minute and slotted his booking in ahead of Claes-Åke's on the schedule. And when Bengt's long-suffering neighbour finally arrived for his own laundry time, there was Bengt, waiting for the last half hour of the Eco-mode cycle to finish.

"Or," Claes-Åke continued, "we could grab a good shovel and dig out the stump. It really doesn't look great at the entrance. It's like saying to any visitor, 'Welcome! This is the neighbourhood where we proudly display our tree stumps for all to admire.' No, Siw and I prefer a bit of order. If you're going to take down a tree, you do it properly, not half-heartedly."

"It's nearly done here," said Bengt, lost in his thoughts and unaware that his neighbour's conversation was more than just idle chatter.

"By the way, did you hear on the news that Sputtovko has landed on Åland? What do you make of that, then? Quite something, eh?"

"*Sputtovko... Sputtovko*!" Claes-Åke exclaimed.

It almost sounded like he had spat the name out.

"But on Åland?" he continued. "I do feel sorry for the people of Åland, I really do. But what's that got to do with the stump?"

"Nothing," said Bengt. "Oh, the stump. Right, I'll sort that out too. If I need help, I'll let you know. No need to worry about it."

*

'One more thing sorted,' Claes-Åke thought contentedly as he made his way back up the stairs. The stump was taken care of, and the laundry was finally in the washer.

Now, all that was left was the rest of the laundry day—tumble drying, ironing, and folding. From Albert's flat, the music was thumping loudly, almost in time with Elaine's hammering on the Megaphone.

'That...' Claes-Åke thought, reflecting on the noise. 'I'll deal with that another day. You can't do everything in one go. Rome wasn't built in a day. Without me, this apartment building would be in a state of absolute chaos.'

Chapter 19

Elaine took in the scene before her. The landscape was breathtaking, with mesmerising shifts in colour created by the varying amounts of snow blanketing the mountain slopes.

She pulled on her thick mittens and snugged her hat into place. It was a distinctive cap in the colours of the Union Jack, extra lined for warmth and a perfect fit. She'd bought it during a business trip to London.

'Wonderful,' she thought as she stood at the edge of Mount Everest. 'Silence. Freedom. How I've longed for this.'

Reaching into her backpack, she unpacked her tent and began assembling it on the spot. The air was icy and crisp, its freshness almost intoxicating. Here, she could finally breathe deeply, escaping the relentless pressures of life and the demands of society.

This was a haven.

Elaine pitched the tent with such swiftness and efficiency that even the most seasoned mountaineer would have been envious. But what was a modern, albeit basic, tent compared to the complex calculations of her scientific profession? A walk in the park, clearly. She also unpacked her primus stove and a folding sun lounger, arranging them neatly and ready for use.

Once she'd finished the most pressing tasks, Elaine sank into the sun lounger and poured herself a steaming cup of hot chocolate from her thermos. The landscape before her was utterly breathtaking. Towering mountain massifs stretched into the sky, their peaks dusted with what looked like freshly fallen snow.

Elaine hadn't experienced silence like this in years.

She sat there for a long time, gazing out at the endless snow-covered slopes. Slowly, the dazzling white of the landscape filled her vision. She half-closed her eyes.

Yes, she thought sleepily, *that's exactly what my aunt used to say: fresh air makes you tired.*

With a contented sigh, she drifted off to sleep.

When she awoke, a biting wind had begun to howl from the east, and the sun was obscured by swirling snow clouds torn up by the gusts.

It was cold—bitterly cold. Elaine shivered and paused to take in the silence once more. Not even the wind could fully disturb the tranquillity.

I hope I brought enough warm clothes, she thought, a frown creasing her brow.

But it really was terribly cold.

*

Elaine was missing. Just as soon as she had returned home, she had disappeared again. Amanda couldn't quite explain how it had happened. The professor's Mini Cooper was still parked outside the apartment building, but there was no sign of its owner. Amanda feared that Elaine was still angry about the Megaphone incident.

Elaine hadn't accused Amanda of any wrongdoing, though. On the contrary, while the other neighbours had heard the full force of Elaine's booming voice, Amanda had been met with nothing but gentleness and patience. Amanda wasn't sure whether to view this as a good sign or not. Perhaps it was as simple as the fact that she and Elaine had formed a bond of mutual understanding. At least, that's how it felt when Amanda reflected on it. She had realised that, deep down, they were quite alike. It was possible Elaine had come to the same conclusion.

In any case, there wasn't much time to dwell on Elaine's whereabouts. The tenants' association meeting was about to start.

The board typically consisted of Claes-Åke, Bengt, and Maja. In any case, Maja had been listed as a board member for several years, though she never actually attended the meetings. The two gentlemen had tried to persuade her to step down from her position, but due to various misunderstandings in communication, Maja remained on the list of board members.

Claes-Åke and Bengt often gave the impression that they had a hand in everything going on in the apartment building, even though Mr. Richardsson always had the final say. This time, however, the situation was somewhat different. The board had called a meeting for all the tenants in the building, and apparently, there were important matters to discuss.

In a room in the basement, right next to the laundry room, there was an office set up. Bengt held the gavel, and Claes-Åke took the seat beside him. One by one, the neighbours began to arrive.

Light poured in through the windows, and the geraniums Siw had arranged on the long table added a cheerful touch. The cuttings were from Mårbacka, brought back from a bus trip the couple had taken there. Claes-Åke had been embarrassed by the geranium cuttings, but Siw didn't think Selma Lagerlöf would mind.

What a burst of inspiration Siw had gained from that trip! She had started a book club, which included Ulla and a few other friends. They had begun with *The Tale of a Manor*, then moved on to *Anna Svärd*, followed by *Gösta Berling's Saga*. This, Siw eagerly announced to the neighbours who had gathered for the meeting.

Small talk is an art mastered by those who have the most, however trivial, things to say, and Siw was in a particularly chatty mood. So much so that Bengt had to bang his gavel on the table to call the meeting to order. Even all the members of Everrock had shown up, with an item on the agenda. The band's presence made the room feel rather cramped. The agenda for the meeting was as follows, and Bengt began reading aloud from his notebook:

1. *Juniper* // Claes-Åke
2. *Noise level* // Claes-Åke
3. *Megaphone* // Everrock
4. *Rent increase* // Amanda
5. *Leaking roof* // Zacharias

Claes-Åke took the lead, having set out the first points on the agenda.

"Well, I got the impression that Bengt was going to remove the stump," Claes-Åke began.

He was quietly relieved that Maja hadn't shown up. If she had, he'd have spent the whole meeting repeating himself like a broken record. Claes-Åke cleared his throat and continued:

"Imagine my surprise when, one morning, I step outside the gate and find a squirrel next to the entrance."

"A squirrel?" Albert asked, incredulously.

"Well, perhaps some of the headbangers in this house have been too self-absorbed to notice, but there's a squirrel, carved out of the juniper stump, right next to the entrance," Claes-Åke said, sharply. "Not to mention that we also live in a music studio that far exceeds the permitted noise levels. I measured it with a decibel meter, borrowed from..."

"Let's take things one at a time," Bengt interrupted. "We can't address everything all at once."

"Excuse me, about the stump," Amanda said, shyly. "But I think it's rather cute."

"Cute!" Claes-Åke exclaimed. "What's that got to do with anything? Have we agreed on which forest creature should be carved out of the stump? Have we had a vote on whether the stump should be removed or undergo the 'renovation' that's just been done?"

"Here's my reasoning," Bengt said matter-of-factly. "Since nature benefits from leaving part of the fallen tree in place, I decided to use both the stump and a number of branches from the juniper. When I put the branches around the stump, I thought a squirrel would complement the scenery nicely."

"It's actually a bit crooked," Siw remarked.

"Honestly, I'm an environmental economist, not a wood sculptor," Bengt said sulkily. "If Richardsson had chipped in a penny, it might have turned out nicer."

"Well, it is what it is," Zacharias chimed in. "Like Amanda, I think Bengt's done a good job. What do you really want, Claes-Åke?"

"I just think we should have had a vote on it, in the true spirit of democracy. I'm not sure we're running some kind of newly established sculpture park here."

"Alright," said Bengt, realising he now had the upper hand.

"We'll vote on it. Who wants to keep the squirrel?"

Several hands shot up. Everyone, except for Claes-Åke and Siw, voted in favour.

"That's settled then!" said Bengt triumphantly. "A victory for biodiversity. Now, onto the third item on the agenda..."

Chapter 20

The items on the agenda were checked off, as was the meeting of the tenants' association. Zacharias had been instructed to call Caspar Richardsson to obtain a statement about his leaking roof. He postponed this monumental undertaking for the rest of the day and for the entire night as well. In the morning, he woke up, noticed it was raining, and donned his raincoat along with a yellow sou'wester that had been passed down directly from his grandfather. His grandfather had owned a fine old wooden boat—a real character of a vessel—and spent much of his time cheerfully bobbing about at sea. The sou'wester, much like the boat, had been a loyal companion, braving countless storms.

As Zacharias stood at the kitchenette, pouring coffee into his thermos to take to the university, he realised that the situation was beyond reproach. Drops from the ceiling plinked steadily into his thermos, one by one. He glanced up, trying to pinpoint the source of the leak, only for a drop of water to land squarely on his thin-framed glasses.

When evening came and Zacharias returned from his studies at the university, he rang the owner of the apartment building. Caspar was seated on his rectangular, metre-long sofa, preparing to enjoy some popcorn while watching television. He carefully rolled up his sleeves to avoid any butter stains.

"Yes, I am, yes," he said, humming sympathetically as Zacharias voiced his complaints about the leaking roof.

"Yes, of course it's unacceptable," Caspar continued. "But, you see, I'm already aware of the issue. It's a real challenge these days to find good builders."

"Really? Builders?" Zacharias replied. "There's a shortage of nurses, doctors, teachers…"

"Yes, thank you, that'll do," Caspar interjected, stifling a yawn. "I've just come from a meeting about all that at the city council."

"…veterinarians, police officers, IT specialists…"

"Vets?"

"Don't you know about the shortage of vets? I thought it was part of the politicians' job to sort out issues like that," Zacharias added, glancing outside as he noticed it had started raining again.

"It was just the other day that I ran into Amanda — you know, my neighbour — at the entrance. She told me that Lou had found a chicken bone in the park. At the very last moment, she managed to get the bone out before he swallowed it, but as the bone was half chewed, she was worried. There was a chance he'd swallowed something anyway, so she took him to the nearest veterinary clinic."

"And then there wasn't a vet available? No, of course not," Caspar said, sounding utterly bored.

"Actually, there was," Zacharias replied. "However, the problem was that…"

"Well, I'm allergic to fur," Richardsson said, clearly wanting to wrap up the conversation. "So I really don't understand all this fuss about animals."

"…anyway, as I was saying," Zacharias continued, undeterred. "When the vet was about to open Lou's mouth to check his throat, he got a nasty bite on his hand. It was completely unexpected because Lou seemed so docile—at least, that's what Amanda said. And then, as the vet was trying to recover from the shock, he muttered something about how Lou ought to show a bit more gratitude, especially given the shortage of vets in the country. I don't think he really meant it—I told Amanda the same, poor thing, because she had tears in her eyes. It must have been the shock talking. I mean, you can't say things like that to small dogs; they don't know any better."

"Have you finished now?" Caspar asked sharply. "I've got an important TV show to watch. In fact, it's quite significant for the future of my political party."

"I was just trying to make small talk," Zacharias replied. "Actually, I wanted to ask you outright when the hell you're going to sort out the roof repair!"

"I'm telling you, the problem is being looked into," Caspar said, clearly offended.

"And when will it be fixed?"

"I'd guess the day after tomorrow, or maybe the day after that. I'm deciding between completely reroofing or replacing some of the tiles. Either way, it's not exactly cheap, I can tell you that."

"And where am I supposed to stay in the meantime?"

"It'll work out. We'll sort something out when the time comes. At the end of the day, we'll get it fixed. One just needs to face each challenge as it comes. It's like running a marathon—you stop at one water station at a time and maintain a steady pace so you don't burn out too early. Like I said, we'll figure something out when the time comes."

"The time is now," Zacharias said, "and I've just about had enough water, thank you."

"Great, excellent. Let's leave it at that..." Caspar replied, pressing the remote control for the TV.

"I warn you, Caspar," Zacharias said irritably. "I'll take this further, if nothing gets done..."

"If you do, I'll talk to you later," Caspar said casually, ending the conversation with a brief "hello". His attention had already drifted. From the TV, which was almost as large as the wall, the intro to the talk show blared.

*

The assistant hurried into Jane's dressing room, only to be met with a scolding—forcing him to leave just as quickly. Once in the corridor, he stopped to adjust his oversized headphones, which stubbornly slid down his head with each movement. He knocked on the door to Jane's dressing room.

No response.

"We'll be rolling soon! I don't want to stress you out, but we're on the clock here!"

A humming sound came from inside, followed by the slow creak of the door as Jane's make-up artist finally opened it.

"Are you ready?" the assistant asked, tapping his pen against the schedule in his hand. He would have much rather grabbed Jane by the arm and shoved her onto the stage. Time was running out. She was later than ever. If Liam carried on like this, he'd no doubt end up with a stomach ulcer. But who would care? The job application had explicitly stated that a stress-resistant stomach was essential.

"Jane?"

"I'm coming, Liam. I'm coming," she replied, standing up from the swivel chair by the mirror. She was in her late thirties by now and relatively well-known. Jane didn't really know how it had all happened – in terms of both age and fame, that is. She had appeared on a few reality shows here and done some modelling jobs there. Time had flown by. Suddenly, she found herself on the popular TV show *Unmask Masked Singer's Salary*, where she had a memorable appearance. And then, voilà! Now she had her own talk show and her own assistant, whose sole purpose seemed to be to annoy her.

Well, Jane thought, *I suppose this is as good as it gets.*

She said aloud, "Move out of my way then. How am I supposed to get to the studio if you're blocking the doorway like that?"

"Oops, I'm sorry!"

Liam quickly moved aside and tapped the schedule with his pen again. The sound was unbearably irritating to Jane. She strode ahead of him into the studio, turned to face the audience, and waved with a big smile before sitting down in her leather-covered swivel chair. She really was very fond of swivel chairs.

She glanced at her papers and waved Liam over, a frustrated frown creasing her brow.

"What's this? They're not in the right order!"

Liam eyed the plastic cards and sighed quietly.

"They were in order before, but I'm sure you've been fiddling with them since."

"No sarcastic remarks, please. Just get them sorted. Now!"

Liam took the cards and stepped aside, quietly sorting them. It took a while, and he could sense the impatience building among the audience and the cameramen. The air was thick with tension. Liam had a sixth sense for that sort of thing—it came in handy in show business, he thought.

"Here," he said, handing Jane the cards. "We're about to start the countdown."

He put on his headphones and stood next to one of the cameramen, holding up his hand to signal the seconds with his fingers. A small red light blinked on the camera.

Jane's smile was dazzling.

"Welcome to my talk show! Today, we have the guests Everrock, Kenneth Hansson, and none other than the bureaucrat Emil Jonsson joining us. It's going to be a great show, isn't it?"

'Great isn't the word,' Liam thought, watching as the musicians from Everrock entered from backstage. He certainly wasn't a fan. *Get this, bring me here, give me...*

'Didn't they learn any manners at music school?' Liam thought to himself.

"I'm so glad you could join us!" said Jane.

"Thank you for having us," Albert replied.

"It's been a busy time for you all. You really made a breakthrough with your song *Dance*."

"Oh, definitely. It's been a whirlwind," said the drummer.

"What's it like singing in English? Do you find it easier to express yourself in English compared to Swedish?"

"Singing in English is great for reaching a bigger audience. But of course, if a song calls for it, we wouldn't rule out singing in Swedish."

"What's the song *Dance* about? What does it mean to you?"

"Quite a lot. We'll always see it as our ticket to the big stages. And it's getting more streams every day..."

"What's the message of the song?"

"For me, it's about truly seeing one another and listening to each other's views," Albert said unexpectedly.

'Sure,' Liam thought. 'The guy sings *'Dance,'* then goes into a heavy instrumental. Real deep. Plenty of lyrics to keep up with.'

"And I hear you've found love this year too!" Jane said, her voice full of enthusiasm.

"Uh, no," Albert said, looking surprised. "I don't think so."

"Yes, I think so," Jane replied, a twinkle in her eye.

"Uh, no," Albert repeated.

"You met in connection to your near-death experience in...?" Jane began, before trailing off. "Oh dear," she murmured, glancing down at her cards.

"Yes, there was an earthquake in the apartment building where I live, but..." Albert started.

Drummer Axel shook his head frantically, knowing it wasn't in their best interest to start discussing anything even remotely connected to the Megaphone.

Chapter 21

"I apologize," said Jane. "My assistant seems to have mixed up my cue cards. How daft!"

She laughed to smooth over the mishap.

Behind the scenes, a studio crew member raised a sign reading 'Applause!' whereupon the audience laughed and applauded, completely out of sync.

"With your newfound fame, what's the oddest thing you've experienced recently?" Jane asked, trying to buy time to sort out the cards.

"You could say a lot's been going on lately" replied the drummer. "For a band like ours, being discovered and having such a breakthrough really means the world to us."

"Sure" said Jane. "I don't know why this comparison comes to mind, but you've really swept through like an earthquake with your music. I wake up every morning realising I have your song stuck in my head."

"We're releasing a new single soon," said Albert.

"Oh, marvellous. That will certainly delight your fans. What's the song called and what's it about? Can you convey its message?"

"It's called *Swing*," replied Albert, "and, well, it's about dancing."

"Lovely! They do say dancing is ever so vital for public health," said Jane.

The audience whistled and applauded. The studio crew member, who had momentarily abandoned his post for a cup of coffee, looked around in surprise.

Jane briefly refocused on her notes.

"We're about to introduce our next guest, coming from a completely different background. Ladies and gentlemen, please welcome Kenneth Hansson, a Member of the Swedish Parliament, currently sparking controversy across social media."

The studio crew member rushed to raise the sign. The audience burst into applause. Hansson stepped onto the stage, dressed in an elegant suit.

Taking the seat opposite the Everrock band members, he adjusted his jacket as he settled onto the cushion.

"Welcome, Kenneth! Before your time in Parliament, you served on the Falköping City Council. While on an educational trip to Cannes, you were entrusted with managing the budget. Today, you're here to tell us what really happened."

"Let me start from the beginning. Every year, we'd head to Cannes for important meetings and a housing construction fair. Absolutely vital for Falköping's future and competitiveness in our ever-globalising world. Now, this has made headline news. Allegations have surfaced about our travel expenses."

"Exactly, it's about you spending five million Swedish kronor of taxpayers' money on your last trip there."

"That's right. And since I had to approve every politician's receipts, it's me who's in the firing line. The media wants to pin it on me."

"But weren't you the one in charge?"

"Not necessarily. It was my job to sign off on the receipts, yes, but of course, I trusted my colleagues. I thought they were too decent to indulge in champagne and bouillabaisse at the taxpayers' expense. Turns out, I was honest—they weren't. Perhaps I was a bit naive. I wasn't particularly fond of these trips myself..."

"No," Jane cut in. "You've mentioned that in several interviews."

"...so, what else was I supposed to do?"

"But now, there's a new twist to the tale. A recent media report claims you were actually behind most of those purchases," said Jane.

"That's not true at all," Hansson replied firmly.

"Allow me to go over the receipts. First, a *robe bleue* for 900 euros. We've received information that your wife was wearing a new blue dress."

"Not at all. Don't you know French? That's a cloak-room fee. Quite pricey, I admit, but considering we were in Cannes..."

"Couldn't you have gone to Alingsås instead?" interjected Albert. "I've heard they host a Festival of Light there, boasting fantastic art installations."

The studio crew member promptly raised his sign again. The audience responded with applause and sympathetic laughter.

"Absolutely not," countered Hansson. "Our main goal was to explore housing construction and the challenges within the industry, not to admire art installations. That would be completely absurd!"

Albert shrugged and was just about to add something when Jane hurried on:

"*L'escargots* for 849 euros."

"Just some sodas. They really charge a lot," Hansson said, as if he'd rehearsed the line in front of a mirror.

"You have to understand," he continued, "I've fought tooth and nail for years to get into the Swedish Parliament, and now my reputation's on the line because of a few receipts for fashion items and chocolate pralines."

"Chocolate pralines?"

"Yes, figuratively speaking."

"How has this scandal affected you?" Jane inquired.

"Significantly. It's a burden, honestly. Every time I do anything, someone brings up a Cannes bill—just like you're doing now. I've moved on from that phase of my life. Now, my constituents and I are focused on the future."

"You've suggested reimbursing 20,000 kronor of that amount."

"Yes, isn't that generous! Out of my own pocket."

"Doesn't that appear rather meager in comparison to five million?" Jane queried.

"That's for the current city council to address. It's no longer my responsibility."

"Thank you for joining us, Kenneth Hansson!"

The audience erupted into applause.

"Last but not least," said Jane, "I'd like to welcome civil servant Emil Jonsson. Last December, he was clearing snow from the roof of his holiday cottage when he suddenly lost his footing and took a tumble. Thankfully, he landed in a sizeable snowdrift with all limbs intact. He's here to share his near-death experience and how it sparked a blossoming romance with his newly divorced neighbour. Meanwhile, let's get Everrock tuned up for their rockin' performance!"

Chapter 22

Zacharias was alone in his flat, feeling thoroughly sorry for himself. On his phone, he was half-heartedly watching his neighbour Albert's appearance on Jane's talk show. Not because he found the interview interesting or even particularly well-conducted, but mainly to remind himself that everyone else seemed to be doing better in life than he was. He could feel his confidence draining away with every passing second.

Still, he realised there was a certain odd comfort in wallowing in self-pity. At some point, you hit rock bottom, and the only way left was up—you had to pull yourself together and sort your life out. That's exactly what he decided to do.

Unfortunately, in his determination, he straightened up too quickly and banged his head on the sloped ceiling of his attic flat, leaving him with a pounding headache. *Great*. Time to think of some practical solutions, he told himself, rubbing his head.

'Well, I did find that dog collar in the park the other day. Maybe I could take it over to Amanda's place, knock on her door, and ask if it's Lou's. When it turns out it's not Lou's (because obviously, it belongs to a much bigger dog, probably a rottweiler), I could chat long enough to casually ask if I can come in for a coffee… you know, given the state of my flat.'

Zacharias paused.

'No, no. That's way too pushy,' he thought, shaking his head.

Then another idea hit him: Elaine had been away for a while. There was no sign she was coming back anytime soon, so why not temporarily move into her flat?

He'd noticed that her door was always left unlocked, as Maja, Bengt, Everrock, and Amanda seemed to come and go freely without locking it. Apparently, Elaine's key was nowhere to be found.

With that, Zacharias packed his things into a rucksack and left the dripping attic flat. Hopefully, this would be enough to put some pressure on his landlord, Caspar Richardsson.

'I've moved out and won't be paying rent until the roof is fixed,' he imagined himself saying.

If he'd had the money, Zacharias would have booked a cheap hotel in a heartbeat. But since his monthly student grant was long gone, he had to get creative.

*

Elaine was fast asleep. Across the snowy plains, icy clouds swept past. Meanwhile, on the side of a cliff, the tops of some mountaineers' caps began to appear above the snow. They moved slowly upwards, and before long, their bulky jackets came into view. The wind howled, and the sun, dim and pale like a low-wattage LED bulb, flickered faintly above the peaks. The climbers pushed themselves to their limits. Their ice axes and the rope binding them together came into sight. One more heave. Now, even the tops of their boots were visible. But Elaine didn't notice any of this. She was still peacefully snoozing in her sun lounger.

The short man, who was bravely going first, coughed.

"Feeling under the weather, Bradley?" asked the taller man, Arthur.

"It's inevitable," Bradley replied. "You can't climb mountains without catching a cold at some point."

"How are we meant to stay socially distanced? If we both end up ill, this record attempt's a bust," Arthur pointed out.

"That's what the rope's for," Bradley said. "As long as we keep to that distance, we'll be fine."

"Hang on—look over there. Do you see that? Someone's on a sun lounger," Arthur said, squinting through the snowflakes settling on his eyebrows.

"You're right," Bradley said, and together they edged closer to the campsite Elaine had set up.

"You! Excuse me!" Arthur called out, giving Elaine a nudge on the shoulder. She jolted awake.

"You shouldn't fall asleep in weather like this," Bradley said, clearing his throat, though his hoarseness remained. "It's minus twenty-eight degrees, for heaven's sake!"

"Why is it that people can't just leave me alone?" Elaine snapped. "What do you want? I'll sleep here if I feel like it!"

"Are you British? Your English is brilliant," said Arthur. "And that knit cap of yours is lovely—such a nice nod to the Union Jack."

"It reminds me of the one I lost," Bradley added. "I tried to find a replacement in the Alps during altitude training, but it was impossible. My theory is it's all down to Brexit. Anything to do with travel or shopping is a nightmare these days."

"You really can't expect to find bobble hats in British colours in Italy," Arthur said. "Personally, I think things have improved since Brexit."

"Improved?!" Bradley exclaimed. "Well, if you think higher prices are an improvement, then I suppose you're right."

"The higher prices aren't down to Brexit, you muppet! It's all about the global situation and the fact it cost us an absolute fortune to leave the EU," Arthur shot back.

"Then why did we do it?" Bradley asked, jutting his chin out. "I'll tell you why—we did it so a locally grown turnip costs £2 instead of £1."

"Have you even been to a shop recently?" Arthur asked. "A turnip doesn't cost £2, and if it does, it's probably because it's locally grown under the EU's organic farming regulations."

"I shop more than you, you pompous get," Bradley retorted. "And by the way, in your world, everything's the EU's fault."

"And in yours, it's all down to Brexit," Arthur snapped, waving his fist at him.

"Who was moaning about the difficulty of getting entry permission because of the new passport rules?" Bradley fired back, coughing.

"That was you."

"Maybe, but you complained just as much."

"I wish we'd never bothered getting that damn entry permit. Then I wouldn't have to put up with you!"

"And I wish you'd gotten the entry permit instead of me. I'd be curled up by a warm fire with my sniffly nose, while you'd be up here freezing all alone."

"Watch the rope, keep your distance!" Arthur shouted. "Don't come any closer, for God's sake!"

Bradley took a step back and happened to glance over at Elaine.

"She's fallen asleep again! This is dangerous—she could end up with frostbite!"

"You! You!" Arthur repeated, prodding Elaine on the shoulder. "We haven't got time to stand here chatting. We need to set up our tent now."

"Get on with it then, but don't bother me," Elaine muttered.

"We're here to break a world record," Bradley said, puffing his chest out proudly.

"Oh, right," Elaine replied. "Does it really have to be on this particular mountain top?"

"We've been planning this for six months, and there's no turning back now. The goal is to stay up here as long as possible—three months is the target. After that, we'll try to get back down faster than anyone ever has."

"And why are you doing this?" Elaine asked, letting out a deep sigh.

"Well, it's obvious, isn't it? Because no one's ever done it before!"

"How do you know that? Maybe a Roman came up here on an outing before our time."

"Ah," Bradley said. "That's possible, but you're missing the point. If that had happened, he would've written it down, and we'd know about it."

"Maybe he couldn't write, or maybe he was just really modest and didn't want to show off. Or maybe he tumbled into a mountain goat on the way down and ended up dead. Or maybe he wrote it on papyrus, but a mountain goat ate it, and then he ran out of money to buy more scrolls."

"Does every one of your theories have to involve a mountain goat?" Arthur asked, struggling with the tent poles as he tried to put them together.

"It's all down to Brexit," Bradley said. "Nobody cares about an Englishman's record attempt anymore. The Europeans just think, *What's the point? Let them carry on with their ridiculous antics.*"

"It has nothing to do with Brexit," said Arthur. "We should be grateful that we're spared the continent's obsession with goats and halloumi. It's like eating rubber – there's nothing to suggest it's even edible."

"What's wrong with halloumi?" Bradley asked, raising a warning finger at Arthur. "I happen to like halloumi."

"No, you don't."

"Yes, I do."

"Last month, during our altitude training in Greece, you said it was the worst invention in living memory."

"Maybe I said that. But I didn't mean it."

"Well, what did you mean then?"

"I was joking! Even you should've picked up on that."

"I didn't."

"No, and you're incapable of setting up a tent properly."

"Alright, I'm getting sick of your insults. Fix it yourself if you're so clever! But I'll tell you, it's a typical EU-made rubbish tent that'll probably collapse any second."

"Made in England, it says," Bradley remarked.

"So it does," Arthur replied. "Still, they could've at least included an instruction manual."

Elaine threw her arms up in exasperation and stood, causing the mountaineers to glance at her in surprise.

"You can borrow my tent, on the condition that you stay quiet. It's heated and everything," she said, gesturing towards the dome-shaped tent.

"Heated? What do you mean, like a sauna?" Bradley asked. Elaine simply nodded.

"No, but that's not possible," Arthur said.

"No," Bradley agreed. "We can't just sit in a heated tent for three months. This is a proper record attempt—at the highest level. One needs to freeze, struggle, despair, fight, and suffer. We can't just lounge in a warm tent, sipping tea for three months."

"Well, don't then," Elaine replied. "But at least think about me. I'm burnt out and in need of some peace and quiet. You can't just go on about Brexit for three months."

"We could talk about something else. I was thinking of discussing the situation in Parliament, for example. It'd be quite interesting to hear Arthur's thoughts on our new prime minister."

"No!" Elaine snapped. "You're not talking about anything."

"Not even politics? Doesn't that interest you?"

"Nothing interests me," Elaine said, flopping back onto her sun lounger.

"But surely something must interest you?" Arthur asked. "Otherwise, I'm starting to think you've fallen into a bit of a depression, and that's really not healthy."

"She's probably just wiped out from the climb," Bradley said. "If not, we'll have to get a psychologist on the phone."

"I don't need a shrink," Elaine said, lying back in her sun lounger. "And you two don't interest me either. So, go ahead and set up your tent, get inside, and zip it shut, so I don't have to listen to you."

Bradley and Arthur, feeling a bit deflated, trudged back to their tent and had another go at putting it up.

"Why didn't we practise this during altitude training?" Bradley asked.

"Because we decided to skip that part. We figured height was the most important thing," Arthur replied.

"Brilliant," Bradley muttered. "Whose genius idea was that?"

*

A few hours later, when Elaine woke up, the two men were gone. Tent pegs were scattered across the snow, a reminder of their earlier presence. Elaine was dressed warmly, but she now felt a bit cold. She looked around and noticed that the mountaineers' tent had been carried away by the wind and had become stuck in a crevasse a few hundred metres away, fluttering like a flag.

When she zipped open her tent and crawled inside, a teapot was immediately thrust toward her face.

"How about some tea?" Arthur asked.

"We were just talking about the latest interest rate hike," Bradley said. "Are you interested in that?"

"No," Elaine replied. "But I'll take a cup of tea."

"I'm guessing you don't have any loans," Bradley said. "That must be nice—no worries! Or you could be like Arthur. No loans, but somehow still finds things to fret about. As for me, I have loans, but I'm not worrying – I'm just letting them marinate for a bit."

Chapter 23

Amanda wandered around Professor Milton's flat in search of a watering can. She was quite absorbed in her own thoughts and didn't notice Albert's presence until she walked right into him.

"Oh, my goodness. I'm sorry" she exclaimed, jumping back in surprise.

"Ah," Albert said, casually. "I just came to borrow..."

He fell silent, glancing around the room before adding:

"By the way, you haven't seen Axel around, have you?"

Amanda replied that she hadn't seen the drummer.

In that instant, footsteps echoed from the hallway, and moments later, Zacharias appeared in the living room.

"Oh, didn't see you there!" he said, caught off guard.

An awkward silence followed. Amanda thought she could hear her own stomach growling.

"By the way," she said. "I noticed a pair of drumsticks on the dresser next to the Megaphone."

And sure enough, there they were. Albert looked at the drumsticks and then around the room, as if waiting for the drummer to show up and start a performance.

"We're about to launch our new song" he said matter-of-factly.

"With the help of the Megaphone?"

"Uh, well, maybe," said Albert.

Amanda's question caught him off guard, and he instinctively raised his voice in response:

"Yes, as a matter of fact! And don't you dare say we're taking the easy road to fame! We've been struggling for ages with nothing to show for it. Don't we deserve to grab the chance when it finally comes our way? Or what?"

"Well..., sure" Amanda stammered, adding:

"I didn't mean to criticize. It's just that Elaine did say no one is allowed to use the Megaphone when she's not at home. And I don't know when she'll be back."

"Oh, whatever," said Albert. "Looks like Axel's already been here. He must have launched our new hit by now."

"So that's what the Megaphone does?" Zacharias said. "Finally, it's starting to make sense. It transmits sound frequencies?"

"Yes," Albert replied. "And you can place the sound wherever you want. If we want to play our music in a shopping centre, for example, we just set the coordinates for that location. Like a GPS, sort of."

"What an invention!" uttered Zacharias in amazement. "It could change the world, and all you're doing is using it for your own gain."

"I knew there would be objections" said Albert irritably. "That's why we've kept it secret."

"Right, that's it—I'm shutting it down, here and now! If Amanda says Elaine's told us not to use it, we'd better listen to her."

"Amanda or Elaine?" Albert asked. "No, seriously, what difference does it make if we use it while Elaine's not here? Are you worried it's going to explode or something?"

"That's exactly what I'm afraid of," Amanda said quietly.

"Just try to stop me!" Zacharias said to Albert. He was, for the moment, on a collision course with everyone and everything. For those who find it hard to imagine such a state of mind, try walking around in rubber boots in your own home for several weeks straight. It seems to encourage a particularly strong 'me against the world' attitude.

Before Albert could wrestle him down, Zacharias had gone up to the Megaphone and started fiddling with its screen settings. He looked for the stop button, and the moment he spotted a red button, he pressed it.

Poff, it sounded, and a bright flash lit up the room, blinding both Amanda and Albert with its sharp light. A cloud of smoke, oddly enough smelling of peppermint, spread through the room.

Amanda gasped for air. She found that particular scent of chewing gum hard to bear. It strongly reminded her of her colleague Rebecca's smacking noises at work.

Next to Amanda, Albert was frantically rubbing his eyes. When they finally regained their vision, they saw that the peppermint-scented smoke cloud was slowly starting to settle.

Zacharias's backpack remained in the hallway, but there was no trace of its owner.

"How terrible!" exclaimed Amanda, sobbing loudly. "What if he has been pulverised?"

"In that case, Elaine and Axel have probably met the same fate" said Albert thoughtfully. "But look on the bright side, at least we haven't been turned into ashes. No, seriously, don't you think it's more likely that he's, well, gone off just like the sound frequencies?"

"Are you saying... he's been teleported?" asked Amanda, looking at Albert with wide eyes.

"I don't know. But that's the kind of thing that happens in the movies" said Albert. "And I prefer to believe in that theory rather than yours."

Chapter 24

At Bengt's home, the TV was on, humming cosily in the background. Bengt was at the stove, making vegetarian meatballs after a long day at work. Pingo, his parrot, perched on the curtain rod, nibbling on a tasty foxtail millet. The parrot's dinner transformed into a cloud of seed husks, gently floating down over Bengt's cooking. The chef was kept busy trying to keep the frying pan free of stray husks.

From the living room and the TV, a voice suddenly announced, *"A strange incident has occurred during President Grumpy's visit to Gothenburg and the climate summit…"*

Bengt's ears immediately pricked up, and he hurried into the living room with the frying pan still in hand. He settled himself on the white sofa, now covered with a grey blanket to hide the coffee and chocolate stains.

On the TV screen, he was greeted by Axel, the drummer, looking utterly bewildered. The band member was being ushered away from a black car by several security guards, all wearing sunglasses.

The newsreader continued:

"A member of the nationally renowned music group Everrock has been arrested today for sneaking into President Grumpy's car. The incident occurred shortly after the presidential plane landed at the airport, when the band member was discovered in the passenger seat of the car intended to take the president to the Swedish Exhibition & Congress Centre."

Bengt's eyes widened in astonishment. His thoughts swirled around his head, much like Pingo's seed husks in the air.

The news report continued with a journalist live from Landvetter Airport. He'd positioned himself right by the check-in desk, surrounded by travellers eager to check in, and was now being swept along by the crowd, as if he were just another piece of luggage.

"These images, captured roughly an hour ago, show the individual who has now been identified as the drummer of the band *Everrock*. This incident has raised a number of critical questions: How did he manage to bypass security and gain access to the vehicle? What were his intentions? And does this signal a major security breach at the climate summit? At this time, many questions remain unanswered."

The studio reporter inquired:

"In what way has this incident affected the president's schedule?"

Amid the bustling scene at Landvetter, the reporter replied:

"This incident has had a significant impact on the president and his team. Reports suggest considerable delays, with the president's speech now postponed. It's still unclear how long the delay will last, as ensuring the president's safety is the top priority before any further arrangements can be made."

The studio reporter then followed up:

"What's the public's response been? What are people saying about Everrock, the band that's taken the music scene by storm?"

The on-site reporter was jostled to the left in the frame by a hurried group of travellers eager to join the check-in queue.

"I have, standing next to me, Vilgot Axelsson... erm, Vilgot? It seems, unfortunately, that we've lost Vilgot for the moment, but perhaps someone else here would like to have a word with us?"

A young man nodded cheerfully at the reporter.

"Right. And what's your name?"

"Axel Svensson."

"Ah, Axel. Just to clarify for our viewers, this is not the same Axel featured in the story. What was your reaction when you heard the Everrock drummer is facing allegations of sneaking into President Grumpy's car?"

"My first thought was that he should've brought his drumsticks with him."

"Oh? And why's that?"

"Well, imagine the possibilities! He could've filmed a music video that would have gone viral, with millions of views, or—personally, I'd go for this option—he could've gently drummed on Grumpy's head. You know, just to see if it really sounds as hollow as you'd expect."

"Right," the reporter said, somewhat awkwardly.

He turned to the studio and said, "Well, at least the people here haven't lost their sense of humour. As you can see, there's certainly no shortage of passionate Everrock fans."

"What?!" Axel's voice shot back irritably from the background. "I'm not an Everrock fan, for heaven's sake. Don't go saying that on the news in front of thousands of viewers."

"Right," said the reporter, looking even more un-comfortable. "So, to sum up, there are plenty of Everrock fans out there, but this one is... well, let's just say, *definitely* not a fan."

In the studio, they'd brought in an expert on American studies, alongside a politician who seemed to leap at every chance to get on TV. It was none other than Kenneth Hansson, the Swedish MP.

"So..." the journalist began, after welcoming the guests. "What effect does this incident have on the summit?"

"None whatsoever," said the expert. "It has nothing to do with the climate summit itself."

"But surely, it must affect the security arrangements?" asked the reporter in the studio.

"To some degree, yes. It's definitely having an impact, but we're not sure yet how significant it is. There's a lot to suggest this could shake things up and even change people's views, but it's far too early to say for certain."

"And you, Kevin Hansson, who's recently been caught up in a scandal over some receipts from Cannes. How does this affect the public's trust in the band, Everrock?"

"Let me put it this way; we know it's having an impact. I've seen how these things can get blown out of proportion. In my opinion, it's just a simple misunderstanding, and I always try to give people the benefit of the doubt. Just as I hope others would do the same for me, I try to believe the best in people. It's highly likely this band member just wanted an autograph from the famous Grumpy. Nothing unusual about that."

"So...," said the studio reporter, turning to the expert. "What's been the reaction in the US?"

136

"Well, I'm probably not the best person to comment on that. I haven't been to the States in years, but as an expert in American studies, I can tell you; according to the media, you're definitely not supposed to believe any of it actually happened. Unless, of course, you're tuning into the more *reliable* news outlets—the ones that would never dream of spreading fake news—and they'll tell you that you absolutely should believe it happened"

"Yes, but this actually happened," said the reporter in the studio. "Are people concerned about the president's security?"

"To some extent, yes," said the expert. "If you believe the incident actually took place, then naturally, you'd be concerned. Or, if you're generally worried about the president, perhaps not. Of course, there are those who think a rock drummer isn't much of a threat to national security, but, well, that's their opinion."

At Bengt's place, the sofa was left empty in front of the blaring TV. Bengt had dashed off to Elaine's flat to take a quick look at the Megaphone. He was still holding the frying pan with the vegetarian meatballs when he bumped into Amanda and Albert at Elaine's.

"What's going on here?" he asked sharply, noticing Amanda's downcast expression.

"It's dreadful," Amanda said. "It looks like Axel and Zacharias have been teleported by this thing. The worst part is, we've got no idea where they are—or if they're even still alive."

"Don't worry," Bengt replied, completely unfazed by the Megaphone's strange behaviour. "Axel's in a bit of trouble with the law, but he's otherwise fine."

He went on to explain what had come out in the news report. Albert wasn't impressed.

"Well, that's our careers done for," he said flatly, before adding, "One minute we're soaring, next we're splatting like a pancake. And seriously, what was Axel doing in Grumpy's car?"

"He probably got too big for his boots," Bengt said, continuing, "I suppose it was just too tempting—having your song on the US President's car playlist as a shortcut to international fame."

"Yeah, sure, that's how you make it big," Albert said, his voice thick with sarcasm. "Axel's totally lost the plot, hasn't he?"

"Well, maybe," Bengt replied. "But let's not forget, Axel's currently a guest of both the Swedish and American police. And there's probably a few secret agents in the mix too."

"That's true! We've got to save him!" Amanda said.

"That's exactly what we're going to do. Let me get settled here with the Megaphone. Right, now I suppose we need to figure out how to reverse the function and teleport your drummer back here."

"I believe Elaine mentioned she was developing the Megaphone," Amanda said. "What if this is what she meant—sending physical matter instead of just sound waves?"

"Exactly," Bengt replied matter-of-factly. "I've used the Megaphone a few times myself, even if it was just for sending sound. Look here, this is an interesting addition!"

Albert and Amanda leaned forward to study a dot moving across the Megaphone's large screen.

"If I'm not mistaken," Bengt said thoughtfully, "that's Axel's position."

"Let's hope so," Albert remarked. "If those are his coordinates, getting him back will be a lot easier."

"We'll give it a go," Bengt said. "Everyone! Take cover, I'm pressing the button... Now!"

Albert threw himself out of the way, managing to drag Amanda with him. It might have looked heroic, but he had actually just got his leather jacket's zipper caught in her cardigan. Bengt shot off towards the kitchen like a bullet. Why he thought it would be safer there than anywhere else was a bit of a mystery.

Poff

A bright flash lit up the room.

Poff

Another flash dazzled Amanda and Albert. Bengt had definitely been right about the kitchen.

"Two Poffs?" Amanda exclaimed, confused.

"And two flashes of light," Albert added.

"That must mean..." Amanda said, hope rising in her voice as she waved away the cloud of peppermint smoke. She gasped for air.

"Axel? Zacharias!"

On the floor, in a heap, the vague outlines of two people were visible. One of them sprang to their feet, his expression one of utter amazement—as if he'd just witnessed a full-on divine intervention.

"Incredible!" Axel, the drummer, yelled. "Quick! Take a photo of me—actually, better idea... get your phone out and do a live stream! Hurry up! I need to make it crystal clear that *I* wasn't the one in that car."

Albert, clearly on board with the idea, followed him over to Elaine's sofa to record the "proof."

"As we speak, I'm in Falköping with Everrock's lead singer, Albert. We've been recording a new song, and I honestly can't believe people think it was me in that car. No chance, right Albert?"

"Definitely not," Albert replied, with the kind of seriousness that only comes with being in on a far-fetched plan. "He's been here the whole time. That would mean someone could teleport between Gothenburg and Falköping in the blink of an eye. Utterly impossible!"

"We're heading out for a walk around Falköping to prove I'm actually here," Axel said, fixing Albert with a determined look. "I'll also show you my driving licence and passport, just to prove it's really me. This is going to be a long live stream, but that's because circumstances require it."

Meanwhile, Amanda had just realised—Zacharias was still missing.

On the floor next to the Megaphone, the other traveller remained, her bright red hair in a tangled mess.

Elaine slowly spun around until she ended up on her back, staring up at the ceiling. She let out a deep sigh, completely oblivious to everyone else in the room.

"Elaine," Amanda said. "You're back! We need your help to find Zacharias."

Elaine didn't say a word. A deep frown formed between her eyebrows as she raised her hands to her ears.

"Not another word," she pleaded.

Bengt stepped out of Elaine's kitchen with a biscuit tin under his arm.

"You've no idea what you've done, Elaine," he said between bites of a crisp biscuit. He eyed his neighbour warily. Most likely, Elaine would jump up and accuse him of tampering with the Megaphone once more. But instead, Elaine, who always seemed to have boundless energy, slowly pulled herself up and shuffled over to the sofa. She lay down again, continuing to stare up at the ceiling. Amanda, after touching Elaine's forehead and hand, soon realised she was both freezing cold and burning up with a fever at the same time.

"She seems to have lost her spark," Amanda said, looking concerned.

"Well, well," Bengt replied. "Maybe you're right. I've never seen her like this, and she's barely said a thing."

Amanda picked up a blanket and wrapped it around Professor Elaine. Meanwhile, Bengt went back to the Megaphone, trying to locate Zacharias. Amanda heard him munching biscuits like there was no tomorrow, and then:

"For heaven's sake! We've got a problem," he exclaimed, rushing back to the sofa. "The Megaphone's completely broken!"

He glanced over at Elaine, still lying there, staring blankly at the ceiling, then added, "Do you think Elaine can help us?"

Amanda shook her head. At that moment, Professor Milton looked a bit like a malfunctioning lamp.

"As you said, we've got a problem—Elaine's completely broken too," she replied, her thoughts wandering to whether they'd ever see Zacharias again.

Chapter 25

Bengt picked up his mobile phone and tuned in to *Timeless Classics – Everywhere, All the Time* on the radio. While waiting for the calming music to soothe Elaine's fragile nerves, he and Amanda sat down on the sofa.

After a while, Albert returned.

"I've had it with Axel and his safety-first obsession," he said. " So, we've taken group photos with every band member, done a live broadcast from Falköping's square, and even swung by the town hall just to check the time on that old clock. And as if that wasn't enough, we ran into Caspar—what a nightmare, by the way—who reluctantly admitted that Axel's actually Axel. Though he only did it after complaining about being late for some 'very important meeting.' But still."

"Well, Elaine's still not available, I'm afraid," Amanda sighed, glancing at their neighbour, who was lying on the sofa, staring up at the ceiling.

Bzzz

"What's that noise?" Albert asked. He followed the buzzing sound along the wall until he reached the kitchen.

Bzzzz

The sound was coming from one of the cupboards. Albert approached slowly, opening it with the suspicion that one of Elaine's inventions might leap out and startle him.

Inside the cupboard, the coffee tin was shaking in time with the buzzing.

BZZZ

Albert brought the tin into the living room.

"Could it be a bee or something?" he asked rhetorically as he removed the lid.

Among the coffee grounds, Elaine's smartphone was vibrating on silent mode.

"For goodness' sake! Why on earth do you keep your phone in the coffee tin?" he exclaimed, before realising Elaine wasn't in any state to respond.

The phone suddenly stopped buzzing and fell silent.

"Who was it?" Amanda asked casually, stifling a yawn as the classical music played softly in the background.

"No idea," Albert replied. "First, I need to get these blasted coffee grounds off the screen. Seriously though, why leave your phone at home when you're going away? And what's the point of putting it on silent if you can't hear it anyway?"

"I don't know," Amanda said, shaking her head. "I think we just need to accept that Elaine's been a little out of sorts lately."

"That's your theory," Albert said. "I'm pretty sure she's like this all the time."

"Oh, seriously?" he muttered as the phone screen lit up. "Someone actually called. Let's see who it was."

Bengt glanced at Everrock's lead singer and said, "Of course someone called. We could hear it buzzing, even though the phone was on silent."

"Zacharias," Albert said curtly.

"Yes, it would be rather splendid if Zacharias decided to call," Bengt replied.

"No, I mean it," Albert said. "Zacharias *has* called."

"Oh, that's wonderful! We've got to call him back!" Amanda exclaimed, springing up from her seat beside Elaine. "How lucky he happened to have his phone on him!"

In tense silence, they waited for Zacharias to answer. Albert held the smartphone, Bengt leaned in to listen, and Amanda hovered close, hoping to catch every word.

Elaine, meanwhile, did nothing at all.

*

"But this is awful!" Amanda exclaimed.

She turned to Albert, who nodded in response, but something in his eyes made Amanda think he found the situation more fascinating than terrifying.

"Isn't it?" she pressed.

"Oh, sure," Albert replied.

He turned back to the conversation on the phone with renewed interest.

"But how on earth did you end up at a lighthouse? Did you set the GPS to some random island or what?"

"I don't know!" Zacharias' voice came through the phone. "I just wanted to switch off that blasted thing! It all went wrong. Alright, I admit it. Happy now?"

"Fair enough, admitting it," Albert said. "So, we've got a starting point. A lighthouse, huh? What does it look like?"

"What does it look like?"

Zacharias took a few steps onto the cliff and gazed at the lighthouse looming before him.

"It's white. Well, whitewashed, to be precise. And the top of the tower's black. Ugh, it's freezing out here."

Amanda had put the phone on speaker mode, and she listened with bated breath. The sound of the strong wind came through, and in the distance, they could hear the waves crashing against the rocks.

"Mhm," Albert murmured thoughtfully.

He seemed deep in concentration, trying to figure out Zacharias' location.

"Tell me," he said, "what's it like around you?"

"Around me? What do you mean? I'm standing on some islet or skerry or whatever you call it, looking out at the sea as far as the eye can see!"

Amanda couldn't stand it any longer. She grabbed the phone.

"Hang in there, Zacharias," she urged. "I promise we'll do everything we can to find you. Just try to stay calm and avoid panicking. Head for the lighthouse and take shelter there. Do you think you can find food and water inside?"

"I think I saw a well nearby. I'll check it out. As long as I have fresh water, I should be alright for a bit. But Amanda?"

"Yes?"

"Don't forget me."

"Never!" Amanda replied firmly. But just as she said it, the call was cut off. She turned to Albert.

"Oh my God! What are we going to do?"

"At least I know what *not* to do," Albert said, his tone matter-of-fact. "We're not turning this into some melodramatic soap opera. It'll sort itself out."

Amanda fell silent, her mind racing. She couldn't help but think that Albert was being unusually cold. Albert, on the other hand, was feeling stronger emotions than he had in quite a while. To his surprise, he realised he was jealous of Zacharias. The reader can decide for themselves why, since the author certainly doesn't know what's so enviable about being stuck at sea on a deserted lighthouse.

But Albert's jealousy didn't last long. Zacharias' plan of surviving on just fresh water for a few days seemed highly unrealistic to Albert, and suddenly, he found himself feeling quite hungry. Since it was hard to feel both envy and hunger at the same time, Albert decided on the latter and began rummaging through Elaine's fridge for something to eat.

Meanwhile, Amanda didn't move. She stood there, deep in thought. When Albert offered her a sandwich with cheese and caviar, she politely turned it down and went to get a glass of water instead.

Chapter 26

It was a beautiful late summer's day, with the sun shining over the town square and the people of Falköping. Claes-Åke wandered around the town centre with a few shopping bags in his hands. He took the path heading home through the park. The sky above him was a clear blue, devoid of any clouds. On Claes-Åke's personal horizon, there were no clouds either. He enjoyed the feeling of being free from worries and problems. Elaine had apparently set off on a long journey for some reason, and Claes-Åke could see the benefits of the current situation.

He hummed softly to an old Springsteen song and sat down on a bench to rest for a while. Before retirement, he had never taken the time to sit on park benches, but he had discovered that there was a certain charm in doing so. Everywhere he looked, there was something new to catch his eye. It surpassed the TV offerings, even though he and Siw had invested in additional channels in their later years.

As Claes-Åke observed a couple walking by with their noisy kids, he felt a sense of relief tinged with nostalgia, knowing that the phase of parenting had come to an end for him, his daughter now grown and independent. When she was younger, she had the energy of a Duracell bunny, ensuring that he and Siw were always kept busy.

The recollection made Claes-Åke take out his mobile and text his daughter to check how she was doing. He used to do so now and then. She was exploring the vast world and traveling to new places. Well, it was as it should be. The fact that their daughter was content and confident suggested that he and Siw had done a commendable job as parents.

When Claes-Åke raised his eyes again, he happened to notice a figure in a suit hurrying through the park with a smartphone and briefcase in hand.

'Caspar Richardsson' noted Claes-Åke. 'I would never give my vote to the likes of him. Though it was rather nice of him to treat us to that tapas restaurant, even if it probably had something to do with Elaine. '

Claes-Åke got up and wandered further through the park, carrying his shopping bags with him. Suddenly, he caught sight of a group of teenagers tossing two soda cans on the ground. It was enough to make Claes-Åke lose his temper.

"Pick up those cans immediately!" he said firmly, standing his ground with such an insistent look that the youths turned around and went to collect the soda cans.

"Well done!" he said when they dropped them in the nearest bin. Much could be said about Claes-Åke, but fair he was.

At the far end of the park, near the flowerbeds and the small pond, the city council had arranged for an insect hotel to be placed. For a moment, he paused, putting his shopping bags down on the ground. Claes-Åke couldn't help but notice that insect hotels seemed to be in fashion these days. He inwardly applauded the initiative. Finally, taxpayers' money was being spent on something sensible.

He eyed the insect hotel but didn't see a single insect. Perhaps they'd been scared off by his appearance and had darted out through the back door. Claes-Åke stepped back a bit and looked at the insect hotel. Then, a lone wasp came buzzing and settled in one of the small nooks. Claes-Åke peered closer at it.

'It's scandalous the way things are,' he thought. 'In the past, I used to get upset about all the wasps that plagued our balcony, but nowadays the whole summer can go by without me seeing a single one of these little rascals.'

He felt a bit guilty when he thought about past summers and how he had dashed around with his fly swatter.

'No, live and let live,' thought Claes-Åke. 'That's the right mindset.'

He took a small portion of his and his wife's coffee cake and placed it in the insect hotel as a peace offering. Then, he picked up his shopping bags and trudged out of the park.

Chapter 27

Steel, concrete, glass, and asphalt. That was Mr. Speakalot's first impression of the Swedish Exhibition & Congress Centre in Gothenburg. He stepped out of the black car as the Secret Service agents held the door open for the president.

Grumpy lumbered out, took one look at the buildings, and sniffed. "I could build taller."

Mr. Speakalot had his doubts. The president's last architectural triumph had been an attempt to break the world record for building a house of cards. Sean still thanked his lucky stars that particular escapade hadn't gone public. Grumpy hadn't even managed to beat Svalbard's record, a feat that was hardly impressive, considering house-of-cards construction isn't exactly a strong suit when you're wearing mittens. The end result stood about two inches high and wobbled if someone so much as breathed near it. Grumpy had sulked for the rest of the day like a child whose balloon had popped. Sean's private opinion? House-of-cards record attempts were the kind of activity reserved for people with zero imagination and too much time on their hands.

Still, at least they'd arrived now.

The climate summit was about to kick off, and Mr. Speakalot was on high alert. He had spare copies of the president's speech stashed in enough places to make a squirrel feel inadequate. Everything had been planned down to the last detail. Naturally, that only meant one thing: something was bound to go wrong. It always did.

"Mr. President, is everything all right?" he asked, his voice cautious. "If there's anything I can do, big or small, just let me know."

"Forget the small stuff, okay?" Grumpy said firmly. "Nobody cares about the details. I'm here to make history—huge history. I'll make sure they remember me."

That was precisely what Mr. Speakalot was afraid of.

*

The outline of a rescue operation began to emerge. Bengt, as it turned out, had made several key deductions:

1. Zacharias was on an island with a lighthouse.
2. The lighthouse was not Pater Noster.
3. The island was uninhabited.
4. Zacharias could hardly have had time to move the GPS far from Axel's original setup, so it was likely he was somewhere in the Gothenburg archipelago.
5. The Coast Guard or the Swedish Sea Rescue Society was not to be involved. How could they possibly explain how their neighbour ended up out there in the first place?
6. They could use Bengt's sailboat, which was moored at Önnereds Brygga.
7. Bengt's electric car could get them to Gothenburg.
8. For reasons that remained unclear, Maja had already taken a seat in Bengt's electric car.

Everything was in place for their departure to rescue Zacharias. But Amanda still had one last thing to sort out—the most important thing of all: finding a dogsitter for Lou. Bengtsson had been kind enough to look after the white fox terrier on a previous occasion, but since he had taken on Pingo, that was no longer an option.

Pingo and Lou didn't see eye to eye at all.

At one point, the parrot decided to bite Lou's ear, probably just to see what it felt like, and after that, Pingo became Lou's worst enemy. No matter how many times Pingo tried to apologise, it didn't help. He even spilled some of his best seeds on the floor in an attempt to bribe the odd four-legged creature. But instead of making peace, the seeds ended up in Lou's face, only fuelling his anger even more. Bengt, for his part, had tried to step in and mediate, but to no avail. In the end, Amanda had to cut her spa weekend short and rush home to collect Lou. So, the idea of Bengt Bengtsson looking after the dog was, quite frankly, out of the question—besides, Bengt was needed for the rescue operation.

Now, for those who aren't familiar with dogs, it's worth noting that the lack of a dogsitter can push even the most mild-mannered dog owner to the brink of madness. This is exactly why, as Claes-Åke was on his way to the laundry, his neighbour stopped him with a request... A request? Hardly! It was more of a desperate plea—almost a demand—asking if he and his wife would be so kind as to look after the lovely little dog.

"Can't your father look after him?" Claes-Åke asked, not exactly jumping at the chance to take Lou off Amanda's hands.

"His new wife is allergic," Amanda sighed.

"I'm afraid I'm a bit prone to fur allergies myself," Claes-Åke said, treading carefully.

"That's strange!" Amanda said, looking puzzled. "But how on earth did you manage to look after Siw's friend's cat then?"

Claes-Åke had completely forgotten about that.

Just last month, he and Siw had been looking after Ulla's cat. If he remembered correctly, he'd told almost everyone in the building about it. And, to be fair, he had quite enjoyed having a cat around. Well, mostly. It had ended badly when the cat decided to treat Claes-Åke's favourite cardigan as its personal scratching post. When he found the poor cardigan shredded on the sofa, he quickly gave up on the idea of ever owning a cat.

"Yes, that's right," Claes-Åke said, having a sudden moment of clarity. "We've promised to look after the cat again this week."

"Oh," Amanda said, lowering her head. "I guess I'll have to take him with me, then. He's not too keen on cats."

"That's right," Claes-Åke said, cheerfully. "Dogs and cats, they just don't mix. It's like cat... and, well, dog."

*

Albert sat in the front seat, while Amanda took the one next to Maja. Bengt slid into the driver's seat of the lime green car and turned to focus his attention on Maja. She sat there, rummaging through her handbag like a woman on a mission.

"What are you doing here?" Bengt asked, sounding rather put out.

"Ugh," Maja grumbled. "Oh, what a thing to say! I reckon it'll be a nice day. Now, you're going to drive me to Gothenburg—I'm off to see my sister."

"I'm not a taxi service," Bengt muttered.

The old lady finally looked up, giving Bengt a puzzled look.

"What's this then? This isn't a taxi!" she said, clearly baffled. "What've you done with the taxi?"

Amanda, ever the diplomat, tried to explain that there weren't any taxis around. Maybe the driver had been delayed? Bengt, however, had a fairly good idea where this was heading.

"Where are you off to, then?" Maja asked, her tone suspicious.

"Gothenburg," Albert replied. He was clearly losing his patience. "Do you want to step out of the car so we can finally get moving?"

"Well done," Bengt said, sarcastically.

"Uff," Maja said. "Gothenburg, is it? Well now, isn't that splendid? Let's be on our way, then."

"Yes, let's," Bengt said, sounding resigned.

"*Vasa*?" Maja asked, using the Swedish expression for 'What did you say?' She uttered the word casually, making no linguistic distinction between the question and Gustav Vasa, the old Swedish king who, according to legend, once took an unexpected detour through the snow on his skis in Mora.

"Nothing," Bengt muttered, turning the key with a sigh. The electric car hummed to life with a soft, contented whir. It gently eased out of the parking space, stretching its wheels like it had just woken up from a nap. With a slight lurch, it rolled smoothly away from the apartment building at 24 Björkgatan, as though the car itself was excited to hit the road, eager for the adventure ahead.

*

Grumpy had just stepped out of his sleek black luxury car outside the Swedish Exhibition & Congress Centre. The queues were long at Korsvägen, and a lime green electric car stood out in the crowd. It was the exact shade of Pingo's plumage.

A white fox terrier gazed out through the open window, looking rather pleased with himself. Amanda had moved him forward to a somewhat hesitant Albert after Maja had complained that the dog was giving her funny looks. Albert had wound the window down slightly, hoping to catch Lou's attention with the view outside. And Lou did spot something interesting — he caught sight of a tuft of hair, bright orange and the shade of carrots. Lou liked carrots.

"Look at that," Amanda remarked, rolling down the car window beside Maja. "Unbelievable! It's the President of the United States!"

Maja seemed to find the whole situation hilarious. She pressed her hand over her mouth and then pointed at Grumpy, clearly amused. Bengt glanced over at the president, who was making his way up the red carpet. Maja burst out with her trademark erratic laugh. The sound echoed across the queuing cars, making its way all the way to Grumpy.

The president stopped dead in his tracks, spinning around and grabbing Mr. Speakalot's sleeve.

"That laugh! It's *exactly* like the one from the Theresa Wilson incident!" Grumpy exclaimed.

Mr. Speakalot rubbed his chin thoughtfully. "I have to say, it does sound rather familiar."

"Speakalot," the president snapped, his voice sharp.

Mr. Speakalot immediately felt a few inches shorter.

"Follow that car!" the president demanded.

"Which one?" asked Mr. Speakalot.

"That bright red one!" Grumpy barked.

"It's lime green, Mr. President."

"Speakalot, I'm telling you—no time to lose!" Grumpy said, gesturing grandly. "Find those saboteurs, and I'll make you the happiest person on Earth. You'll get huge rewards—the best rewards. But mess it up, and... *poof.* It's over. You won't even believe how over it is."

"I was fired last week, remember? Are you firing me again?"

"If that's what it takes, absolutely," Grumpy replied with a sneer.

Mr. Speakalot sighed and did what was required of him. He climbed into the black car and told the driver to follow the lime green one. As they drove off, he couldn't help but wonder what would happen to the president's big speech at the climate summit—and whether, after months of loyal service, the president had mistaken him for one of the Secret Service agents.

Chapter 28

The moment had arrived for Grumpy to give his big speech at the climate summit. He was accompanied by a group of security guards as he ascended the escalators to the designated floor. The escalator became crowded with the president and his staff. Grumpy extracted his speech manuscript from his pocket, briefly scanning the first pages. Suddenly, probably due to his age and the height difference caused by the journey, he temporarily lost his balance.

The papers were sent flying in every direction. Some got caught in the moving handrail, which was speeding ahead of Grumpy. The pages were swept up the stairs and into the escalator system. Several sheets got caught between the steps and were torn to shreds.

On the upper floor, an elderly lady managed to catch half a sheet of paper. She offered the damaged page to the president when he finally stepped off at the designated floor.

"Is this all that's left?" Grumpy asked, his voice tinged with frustration as he grabbed the piece of paper from the lady. She must have seemed utterly harmless, with her hand-knitted handbag, as none of the security guards objected.

"Indeed, that's all there is. Quite an unfortunate mishap, don't you think? Did you lose your balance?" she queried, scrutinizing him cautiously over her horn-rimmed glasses.

"No" Grumpy said firmly. "Losing my balance isn't something I do. "

"Well, it's only natural. Especially as one gets older, you know. "

"Not for me," said Grumpy, gazing broodingly at his half sheet of paper.

"Well, did you really need to run for presidency at your age? I would recommend starting a rose garden instead and indulging in that."

"How did that lady get in here?" Grumpy asked loudly. One of his staff replied that they had no idea.

"I'm here for the annual book fair" announced the lady. "There usually are so many different genres, but this year it seems like everything is about the climate crisis. But that's also an important topic, of course."

The president left the lady with the hand-knitted bag without a word in response. Then, he called for Mr. Speakalot to bring him a copy of the speech. It was at that juncture that Grumpy realised he had mistakenly sent Mr. Speakalot on another errand.

Finally, Grumpy ascended the speaker's podium. There was no sudden, enthusiastic outburst of cheers from the audience. One just leaned back to see what foolish things the president would come up with this time. President Grumpy lived up to his reputation. At this point, without any involvement of the Megaphone.

"Nature..." he started. "It's a big deal, folks. Really big. And you know what? We're all here because we've underestimated just *how* big it really is. Personally, I've done just fine without nature—always have. But let me tell you about something that really hit home on my trip to a zoo in the UK. Big, big zoo, by the way. I saw this huge brown bear, and you know what that made me think of? Winnie the Pooh. You know, the famous bear from England. Everybody loves him. And what's he always doing? Eating honey, right? But, folks, let me tell you, it's not good for a bear to eat that much honey. Not good at all."

He paused dramatically for effect, letting the crowd hang on his words before continuing:

"But here's the kicker: when I was at the zoo, the experts there tell me something unbelievable. They say bears—actual bears, not cartoon ones—don't eat honey like Pooh. No, no. They're all about blueberries and such. That's right. Blueberries, folks. Much healthier."

In the audience, people exchanged confused glances.

"Does any of this actually mean anything?" the lady with the hand-knitted bag asked a journalist. "I know he's the President of the United States and all that, but I definitely won't be buying his book."

Grumpy straightened up, then leaned forward onto the podium with a relaxed posture.

'I'm a total master of improvisation,' he thought. 'Let's see what genius ideas pop into my head next.'

"So, here's the thing: Winnie the Pooh? Fake news! Total fabrication, folks. He's not real. He's just a bunch of made-up stories. Now, listen, we need to do our part for the climate, right? But let's be honest, the climate owes us something too. That's why I told you about my visit to that zoo in the UK. What has the climate ever done for us? I want answers, folks. Let's talk about it right here at this climate summit. What has the climate ever done for us?"

"Thank you" said Grumpy, then leisurely stepped down from the speaker's podium. With that, the speech had drawn to a close. *Grumpy had left the building.*

"They're always shorter in real life than they appear on TV" said the elderly lady with her hand-knitted bag.

Chapter 29

The sea was unusually quiet, and a solitary white cloud drifted slowly across the clear blue sky. Within a few hours, Sputtovko had been picked up by a luxury motorboat, and Åland was now far behind them.

"Extraordinarily... hrm... bad treatment from the people of Gothenburg," he said to one of the minions.

The minion in question nodded and glanced down at the chart, clearly keen to change the subject. Efforts had been made to explain to Sputtovko that they were still quite a distance from the west coast, but the leader stubbornly insisted that Åland was, in fact, Gothenburg. And if Åland was actually Göteborg, then the island of Brännö wasn't far off at all. The climate summit would have to wait. There were more pressing matters to deal with now.

The secret operation that Sputtovko's intelligence service had initiated seemed to have gone awry. To the minions' misfortune, their leader had overheard about the failure in the boat's radio communication.

"Catastrophic!" Sputtovko muttered to himself, standing next to the captain. "These incompetent idiots! Did you hear me say idiots? Yes, I take this very seriously. Spilling coffee on the instructions! That just can't happen."

"It can happen to the best of us," said the interpreter, his words hanging in the air as he realised he was no longer needed, his presence feeling more like a formality than anything useful.

"Or, er, I mean: it *only* happens to the worst," he continued, flustered. "That's what I mean. It happens to the worst, but never the best. Definitely not the best."

"Really? And who is *best*?" asked Sputtovko, puffing out his chest proudly.

"Well, it's you," said the interpreter, bowing quickly, though it looked more like he was trying not to fall over as the boat rocked.

"Hrm," Sputtovko grunted, looking pleased with himself. Then his expression soured.

"How you steer this thing, you amateur pretending to be captain?" he snapped.

The captain glanced sullenly at the chart.

"There's coffee on the chart. It'll be hard to navigate now," he muttered, shaking his head as if it were the most tragic thing to ever happen on his watch.

Sputtovko shot a glance at the coffee cup in his hand, then at the dark brown stain spreading across the chart, his face turning crimson.

"What is this madness? The boat is shaking like it's in a blender! Fix it, now! Anyone can spill their coffee when the sea's this rough! Does captain even *know* the price of coffee these days? Do you want to destroy me? This is treason! You are ruining your one true leader!"

He spun around to one of the minions, his eyes narrowing. "Is this *traitor* on the list?"

The minion, looking like he wasn't entirely sure he was still alive, nodded quickly.

"Yes, yes, let me check. I write down, uh, this *amateur pretending to be captain*."

"Good!" said Sputtovko.

He sipped his leftover coffee and added:

"Very good!"

"Well," the interpreter said meekly, "if I'm getting this right, our agents seem to remember the island's name having four letters. How about we try Hönö? I can see it here on the chart, rather than Brännö?"

"No," Sputtovko snapped, waving his hand dismissively. "My gut says this *scorched* island is much better. Tell them to look there! And as for this so-called 'captain'—turn this boat around! I'm done with this madness!"

"If the fuel's enough to get us there, that is," the captain muttered.

"Ah, don't bother me with such petty, *how you say*, details!" Sputtovko scoffed.

"And our water tank is empty," the captain continued.

"Ah, well, now that the captain mentions it, I am *very* thirsty," Sputtovko said.

"We're out of coffee," the interpreter added.

"Then, grab water from sea!" Sputtovko snapped. "Stop fussing over irrelevant, *how you say*, details."

"But... it's dangerous to drink seawater," the interpreter said, confusion in his eyes.

"Nonsense!" Sputtovko growled, his voice dropping to a dark, threatening tone. "Is *fake news*! Lies, yes, lies from people who want us to die of thirst, on great, mighty sea! Cowardly germs, the lot of you! Is there no one here with the guts to take a sip? What, did you think you'd swell up like a balloon and pop? Give me a drink! Right now! I'll show you all!"

The interpreter fetched a crystal glass and leaned over the railing, filling it with seawater. He handed it to Sputtovko with a skeptical look on his face.

The corpulent leader downed the glass in one go, then looked around at his subordinates with a triumphant grin.

"Haha! What did I tell you? The taste is delicious. I've just ingested some very beneficial vitamins and minerals while you lot stood there, thirsting like fools!"

To emphasise his point, he gulped down ten more glasses of seawater, as the minions stared, eyes wide with disbelief.

"That's not healthy," the captain said. "We might need to change course."

The captain turned to the interpreter, raising an eyebrow. The interpreter glanced at Sputtovko and gave a quick, nervous nod, as if confirming the inevitable doom.

"Urk," Sputtovko muttered, his face turning a sickly shade of green, almost matching the colour of his tie.

*

All roads may lead to Rome, but none seem to leave Gothenburg. After circling Korsvägen a few times, bumping over a kilometre of cobblestones, stopping at about ten sets of traffic lights, and making a U-turn towards the central station, the lime green car somehow ended up in a tunnel. Then, without so much as a protest from Bengt's GPS, they turned off near Järntorget, a central square in the city.

"It didn't look like this before," Bengt remarked.

"No, thank goodness for that," Albert replied.

"It's mostly the hotel that's newly built," Amanda said, her eyes fixed on the tower stretching up into the sky.

"Make a U-turn!"

Even GPS Ingrid was beginning to lose her patience.

"And how exactly am I supposed to do that?!" Bengt exclaimed.

"I said I'm going to visit my sister in Frölunda," Maja clarified from the back seat.

In the following car, Mr. Speakalot sat lost in thought.

'They don't seem to have the faintest idea where they're going. How very odd. Quite mysterious,' he pondered.

He'd figured out that the strange laugh came from the elderly lady in the company. When the electric car in front finally arrived in Frölunda and the lady stepped out, he asked the driver to stop. Speakalot got out and ventured into the well-kept residential area, discreetly following the silver-haired lady. Maja, in the meantime, was oblivious to the president's advisor. She slowly made her way to her sister's front door, leaning on the railing as she used her cane to ring the doorbell. A plump little lady opened the door and smiled broadly.

"So, you came after all, my dear!"

"Uff," Maja muttered, shuffling into the hallway.

"Who's this you're with?" her sister asked.

Speakalot realised he'd been spotted, despite his best efforts to remain unnoticed.

"My dear ladies, I was wondering if I could ask you a few questions?" he said with great dignity.

"Oh, I do think we've got someone from the Office for National Statistics here with us!" Maja's sister said cheerfully.

"Just ignore him. He'll probably go away," Maja muttered, giving the sharply dressed man a wary glance.

"Statistics help us understand where society is heading and how we can best prepare for the future," Maja's sister said, sounding like she'd read it straight from a government leaflet.

"*Welcomme*," she said, welcoming the president's advisor inside. A table was laid with seventy different variations of the classic seven types of biscuits. Mr. Speakalot quickly realised he had a particular weakness for Brussel biscuits—yes, a Swedish culinary classic, despite the misleading name. He couldn't help but suspect the president's taste in biscuits would be a tad more... patriotic. For now, however, Speakalot was thoroughly content sitting at this table in Frölunda with the plump, jolly sister and the decidedly less jolly other sister, happily munching on *Brysselkex*.

Chapter 30

"Well, this boat's having a bit of a wobble today! Oho, oho, ahoy!" shouted the gourmand Bergling from the lighthouse as he uncorked a bottle of champagne. The cork flew far over the rocky outcrop below. Meanwhile, Zacharias was fixing the lens of the lighthouse beacon. Bergling's entrance into the story had been as sudden as it was chaotic. Zacharias had been standing atop the lighthouse when he spotted a shiny, fast motorboat. Naturally, he waved his arms frantically, shouting for rescue. To his great luck, Zacharias saw the motorboat change course. The skipper waved back and steered towards land.

"*Hooow* did you end up there?!" shouted the motorboat's owner, continuing to wave his hand as though signalling with a torch. Zacharias couldn't hear anything, for obvious reasons. The skipper shouted even louder as the island's cliffs loomed closer. Zacharias yelled back, but, once again, the skipper didn't hear him... for obvious reasons. And, as one would expect, the motorboat ran aground on the rocks. The skipper shouted even louder.

Thankfully, Zacharias was a strong swimmer and managed to get the distressed man out of the water. As they caught their breath on solid ground, a few bottles began to float towards the shore.

"Well, that's one for the books!" exclaimed the owner of the stranded motorboat. "Another near-disaster averted! Champagne! Shipwrecked or not, we'll still have everything we need! Allow me to see if I can retrieve some more of the cargo. I've also got a pretty sizable stash of sourdough biscuits. They're delicious! Let me just..."

"Wait a second. What's your name, and who are you?" asked Zacharias.

"How rude of me," said the well-mannered gentleman, throwing his arms out. "Allow me to introduce myself! Bergling. Gourmand by profession. Pleasure to meet you."

And that, as they say, was that.

Zacharias had eaten his fill of biscuits, and Bergling had drunk himself silly on champagne. Meanwhile, Zacharias couldn't help but berate himself for not giving clearer instructions to Amanda and Albert.

'Why didn't I think it through?' he groaned to himself. 'I could've at least mentioned the little red shed by the lighthouse. Maybe said something about how big the island is... but no, of course not. How daft can one be? Typical of me to end up with a champagne-chugging opera singer. Just brilliant!'

"Are you pondering something, Zick-Zack?" asked Bergling, casually waving the champagne bottle in a zigzag, as if to match the nickname.

"I was just thinking, the last thing to leave a man is hope," Zacharias said.

"Oh, it's far too early to despair," said the gourmand Bergling, half-joking. "When the sourdough biscuits, cheese, and champagne run out, that's when I'll despair like never before. Would you care for a glass?"

"No thanks," Zacharias replied firmly. "I need to keep my wits about me if I'm going to sort this out."

"There's no way that's possible!" Bergling exclaimed, then added, "Oh yes, I suppose it takes a statistician to work out the electronics... Can't you hear how ridiculous that sounds? Stop messing with that before you get a thousand volts through your body! Instead, let me tell you about the time I found a pink pearl in an oyster. It was during a stay in Paris in the '80s..."

"Hold on a minute!" Zacharias interrupted. "Did you say something about cheese?"

"Did I forget to mention that?" Bergling asked, frowning. "I found a stash of waxed cheese in the red shed by the lighthouse. It was in perfect condition, with a distinct note of pickled walnut. Absolutely brilliant!"

"And you didn't think to tell me? No wonder you're in such a good mood. Am I meant to survive on water and biscuits while you feast on waxed gourmet cheese?"

"Well, it doesn't taste great with the wax still on, you'll need to remove that. By the way, it was a bit mouldy in the middle. One doesn't want to get in the habit of serving mouldy food."

"This isn't the Nobel banquet!" Zacharias replied. "You make do with what you've got."

Bergling seemed lost in thought.

"Strange, really..." he muttered to himself.

Zacharias looked at him questioningly.

"Well, that mould in the middle of the cheese… it was white mould, but still, not..."

"Spare me the mould talk, please!" Zacharias cut in.

"And there were plenty of plastic bags there as well," Bergling went on. "We've all heard about the plastic problem in the oceans, but I never imagined it would start making its way into cheese, of all things. It's a bit alarming when you think about it, isn't it? Imagine enjoying a nice Saint Agur from the Alsace region and then suddenly finding a plastic bag with white mould in it. Picture choking on that bag, struggling for breath, and nearly having a panic attack. Then a kind passerby doctor steps in and has to perform some emergency life-saving manoeuvre. And as if that wasn't bad enough, from then on, blue cheese will never taste the same to you!"

"I think we have somewhat different ideas about what makes life worth living," Zacharias remarked, giving the gourmand a pointed look. He adjusted his steel-rimmed glasses and stared thoughtfully at the lighthouse.

"Well, I suppose you'll have to show me the waxed cheese, Bergling."

"Indeed," the gourmand replied, suddenly looking rather melancholic. He seemed almost reluctant to share this magnificent batch of well-aged delicacies with someone who might mistake a humble cottage cheese for a work of fine art.

Out on a nearby islet, some harbour seals basked lazily in the sun, watching calmly as the two castaways made their way down the cliffs towards the red-painted shed. On the beach, one could see cow parsley scattered around, along with patches of red clover.

The sun was setting, with hours still to go before dusk. Just as the statistician and the gourmand disappeared into the shed, a sailboat drifted by without a sound.

"Look!" Amanda cried, leaning over the railing.

"Seals!"

"Hmm," Albert murmured absent-mindedly, eyes fixed on the GPS screen beside Bengt at the helm. Amanda glanced over her shoulder and asked the others:

"Shouldn't we stop at this lighthouse?"

"No," Bengt replied. "It's off my planned route. We'll start with the King, then take one lighthouse at a time heading straight north."

"The King?"

"The King, the islet *Kungen,* lies just west of the coastal town of *Lerkil,*" Bengt explained. "Kungen has a white and black lighthouse. Seems as good a call as any."

"I'm not so sure," Amanda said softly. "But something tells me this islet is worth checking out."

Suddenly, a motorboat shot past the sailboat at high speed. Bengt raised his fist in the air and shouted curses at the speedsters. Amanda let out a startled gasp as the sailboat tipped sideways in the waves. Albert held on to the boom to steady himself, while Bengt gripped the helm firmly. Lou, at the bow, braced himself against the rocking of the boat. Amanda had dressed him in a sturdy dog lifejacket, bright red, which she had borrowed from the harbour office.

"Bloody hell, what a bunch of villains!" Bengt bellowed. "No electric motor, mind you. Some people do everything they can to pollute the archipelago with fumes. Black speedboat, black-rimmed sunglasses – typical mafia types!"

In the lighthouse, Bergling and Zacharias were arriving at the same conclusion. The gourmand held up a half-eaten wedge of cheese, in the middle of which was a tangle of plastic bags.

"Look," said Bergling. "And inside, there's white powder from mouldy cheese. White mould. Well, we can eat around it for now. Until we're rescued."

"Erm," Zacharias coughed. "I'm starting to worry this isn't white mould."

"Salt, sugar?" Bergling suggested.

"Thank God you didn't eat this too," Zacharias replied.

"Gelatin powder, or maybe that vegetarian version. What's it called again?"

"You'd be dead as a rock by now," Zacharias said, throwing the cheese wedge aside with a disgusted look.

"That's interesting," Bergling remarked. "In Swedish, we say *'död som en sten.'* Did you know they say *'dead as a dodo'* in English? It refers to a bird, the dodo, from Mauritius that went extinct a few hundred years ago."

"Did it?" Zacharias asked. "If those crooks get here before we leave the islet, we'll probably be as dead as a dodo too."

"No, no," Bergling said firmly. "We can't just translate the expression literally. The English chose the dodo; we should pick something else. If we're going to localise it, maybe we should reference a Nordic prehistoric animal. How about *'dead as a mammoth'*? It has a certain finality to it."

"By the way..." Bergling began, first eyeing the last wedge of cheese, then turning his gaze to Zacharias. Suddenly, the gourmand started to stutter uncontrollably.

"You don't mean... Oh, my God. Not that... I'm not religious, but... you don't mean..."

Zacharias nodded gravely, his face serious as he looked at Bergling. The gourmand, in turn, went as white as the cheese, looking like he might collapse into a heap at any second.

"A rogue state, perhaps… or a mafia gang, or some madman," gasped Bergling. "I… I'm too young to die!"

Chapter 31

After much back-and-forth, Zacharias had managed to calm the gourmand Bergling down, and the hard work of constructing a stronghold at the top of the lighthouse began. It was just in time. Slowly, the twilight settled over the surrounding sea and island when a black motorboat appeared on the horizon. The sound of the engine grew louder as the seafarers neared their destination. Bergling pointed with a trembling hand at the crew, all of whom were wearing black sunglasses. With his other hand, he clutched a bottle of champagne and pressed it tightly against his chest.

"Duck," urged Zacharias, as he adjusted a wooden crate in front of the door. "We mustn't be spotted."

Bergling ducked and peered towards the island's cliffs. The motorboat slowed down and carefully glided towards a sheltered cove on the eastern side.

The gourmand turned to Zacharias and exclaimed,

"They're after the waxed cheese. What if they notice one of the crates is missing?"

"We'll have to take the risk," Zacharias replied.

"That's true, we definitely don't want to starve if the siege drags on," Bergling agreed thoughtfully.

"I was actually thinking we needed something heavy to block the door," Zacharias clarified.

At that moment, the unwelcome visitors became visible next to the lighthouse.

"They're getting closer," Bergling breathed, unwrapping his sandwich with a nervous rustle of wax paper.

"Please, don't eat now," Zacharias whispered.

He gestured for Bergling to put the sandwich down.

Suddenly, a faint creak sounded as the door on the ground floor opened. Bergling took a bite of his cheese-topped baguette.

"I have to eat so I don't die of fear," he murmured between bites.

The lighthouse seemed eerily quiet. Zacharias gestured once again for Bergling to maintain silence. Bergling chewed even more quietly. Voices began to drift up from the ground floor. It was impossible to make out what was being said, but the voices sounded irritated.

"Ouch!" Bergling exclaimed sharply, looking down at his sandwich with a horrified expression. "I think I've broken a tooth. What on earth is this? A chip of some sort?"

Zacharias made his way over to him.

"A USB drive," he noted. "With the military's logo on it. So, we're dealing with foreign spies. And I assume you found that sandwich in the red shed, did you?"

"Well, how did you know that?" asked Bergling.

"What a disaster!" sighed Zacharias. "We're done for."

Both he and the gourmand jumped as muffled footsteps began to echo from the stairs. While Bergling clutched his unopened bottle of champagne, Zacharias began scooping the waxed, round cheeses from the crates. He then opened the door to the staircase and hurled the first one with all his might. A loud shout and a thud echoed as the cheese hit its target.

Instantly, chaos erupted in the lighthouse. The sound of running footsteps and raised voices came from the ground floor. Suddenly, one of the men appeared on the upper landing. Zacharias continued to hurl more cheese, which rolled down the stairs at full speed, causing the attacker to lose his balance and tumble back down.

Meanwhile, Bergling's nerves had spiralled into full-blown hysteria. He screamed for help, and in his frantic state, accidentally triggered the foghorn. The noise was so deafening that every ship within a ten-mile radius could hear it, including a certain sailing boat.

Zacharias found himself face-to-face with yet another attacker wearing sunglasses. In that instant, it hit him with horror that they had run out of waxed cheese.

Without warning, a loud popping sound rang out behind Zacharias. A champagne cork shot into the air and struck the attacker square on the forehead. The man staggered, wobbling for a moment before falling backwards and landing in the empty crate.

Bergling quickly slammed the lid shut.

*

A little later, Bengt's sailboat arrived at Valö. Albert, the first to set foot on shore, spotted a black motorboat speeding away over the waves from the east side of the island. Making his way up the lighthouse steps, he stumbled upon some unconscious individuals with their sunglasses askew and a large amount of waxed cheese.

Once the Coast Guard had been called, Amanda, Bengt, Albert, and Lou mustered the courage to make their way to the top of the lighthouse. Zacharias nearly collapsed into the arms of his rescuers, on the verge of tears. Amanda, looking worried, exclaimed:

"Poor you. It must have been dreadful being stranded on a deserted island like this."

"Deserted?!" Zacharias repeated. "If only it had been that simple..."

"Good day," came Bergling's voice, as he swung himself off the lid of the wooden crate and eagerly shook hands with his rescuers. "Bergling. Gourmand by profession. Pleased to meet you!"

Chapter 32

The weather was utterly delightful, with the sun shining beautifully over the lawn at 24 Björkgatan in Falköping. Even an artist who favoured blue could not have painted a sky that blue. Dandelions were piling up around Bengt's crooked sculpture by the entrance. Pingo had been allowed out into the greenery, and the green parrot now rested proudly between the ears of the wooden squirrel.

In an attempt to offer some relaxation to the overly-stressed Elaine, the neighbours had come up with the idea of organising a picnic in the garden. Elaine was kept in the dark about the plans until she found herself sitting in a deckchair outside the apartment building.

It wasn't entirely clear who had organised the picnic. Regardless, the picnic idea had quickly gained momentum, spreading from neighbour to neighbour at lightning speed. Eventually, everyone in the entire building was involved in the preparations. To everyone's slight surprise, Albert had also appeared in the local shop where Amanda worked, offering to help buy food and drinks.

Or, as Albert put it:

"Need a hand with anything? I thought I could, like, carry the bags. And seriously, this shop's rather cramped, I could probably walk around it three times in a minute."

The gum-chewing Rebecka nearly choked on her gum when she spotted the famous singer. Between chews, she flirted with Albert and somehow found time to give Amanda a bit of a telling-off for not mentioning her "celebrity mate" sooner.

Amanda, somewhat taken aback by the situation, carried on shopping, though her actions were now a bit more distracted. After strolling down the aisles and picking up everything from pineapple to garlic, caviar to salmon, Albert started taking charge of the shopping. In the end, they gathered all they needed for the picnic, plus enough to host a banquet.

At the checkout, Rebecka greeted them with all the enthusiasm she could muster. She didn't stop talking for a second, and in all that chatter, she accidentally swallowed her chewing gum. Amanda stepped in and gave her colleague a friendly thump on the back. Once Rebecka had regained her breath, she continued talking as cheerfully and eagerly as if nothing had happened.

It wasn't just Albert and Amanda helping out with the picnic preparations. Bengt had also gone off to do some shopping. Although he didn't drink, he still had a suggestion to offer at the tenants' association's last-minute meeting.

"I'm going to mix a colourful drink for Elaine," he had declared. "The effect of a colourful drink shouldn't be underestimated. I had a great-grandfather who was on his deathbed at the age of 89, but one daiquiri from my great-grandmother, and he was right as rain. Just like that. 'Hey, hup!' he shouted, and before she could even put the rum bottle down, he was up and out of the sofa. And just to clarify, he was a strict non-drinker every other day of the year, my great-grandfather."

At this point, Bengt looked very pleased with himself and then concluded with the words:

"Now, thankfully, Elaine isn't on her deathbed, but depression is a tricky thing. If good food, a couple of drinks, and good company can't lift her spirits, then I don't know what will!"

Both Siw and Claes-Åke were looking forward to the picnic.

"After all, when you think about it, it's certainly in the spirit of good neighbourly relations,' Siw had remarked to her friend Ulla over the phone. "But Elaine is such an odd one. I've never quite figured her out. One day she's as happy as a lark, and the next, she's as prickly as a pebble in your shoe."

With Zacharias lending a hand, Claes-Åke unearthed the kettle grill from the chaotic storage room of their apartment building, digging it out with the precision of an archaeologist. Siw noted that the once-black metal frame was now grey with dust.

"A bit of dust never hurt anyone," Claes-Åke quipped, puffing away a thick layer from the grill.

Unfortunately, the gust hit Zacharias, who had to pause and clean his glasses, which were now covered in dust.

"Claes-Åke!" Siw exclaimed, clearly irritated. "Can't you be a bit more careful? Just look at the mess you've made!"

Claes-Åke looked around, baffled, as Siw bustled over to Zacharias, stopping him from wiping his glasses on his sleeve.

"You'll ruin the lenses like that," she chided. "You need a proper cloth. Come on, I'll get you one."

Then, turning to her husband with a pointed glare, she added, "And you, in the meantime, can give that kettle grill a proper clean—with soap and water."

Claes-Åke opened his mouth, ready to protest, but Siw swiftly cut him off.

"…and don't you dare try to tell me that a bit of dust is good for the stomach!"

Claes-Åke promptly closed his mouth, thinking better of it.

The temporary troubles with the kettle grill, unfortunately, didn't end there. After Zacharias' glasses and the grill had been thoroughly cleaned, an unexpected discovery was made.

Zacharias noticed a small strip of paper sticking out from the Erikssons' Persian carpet.

"You might have dropped this… looks like a receipt, I think," Zacharias said, bending down to pick up the paper and passing it over to Siw.

Siw quickly realised it wasn't a receipt. It was a label that read *Made in China*.

Siw drew her own conclusions, which led to a stern fifteen-minute "chat" with Claes-Åke. The "chat" quickly escalated into another fifteen minutes of raised voices, followed by yet another fifteen minutes of tears, dramatic sighs, and a lot of "why me?" By this stage, Zacharias had taken the reins of the barbecue. Claes-Åke, who'd carelessly ruined his wife's inherited, delightful, and—crucially—genuinely Persian carpet, was sentenced to an hour's house arrest. Siw, meanwhile, had decided she was still going to the neighbour's gathering and picnic—just not with her deceitful husband in tow.

The observant reader might wonder if the picnic was really worth all the hassle. Elaine found herself thinking the same. Once the preparations were finally done, a somewhat grumpy but pardoned Claes-Åke managed to get her settled into a deckchair on the lawn in front of the apartment building. Unable to keep it to herself, Elaine blurted out:

"What's the point of all this?"

The deckchair was placed next to some beautiful picnic blankets that Bergling had brought along to the event. With dramatic gestures and a voice booming like a stage actor, Bergling passed the grilling duties to Zacharias for the Camembert he'd bought.

Zacharias, not exactly a grilling pro, suddenly found himself hit with a serious case of performance anxiety. Without realising he was adding to the pressure, Bergling casually revealed that the Camembert had cost him £533 per kilo.

"I must admit, it's been an absolute delight to meet such remarkable individuals as yourselves!" Bergling exclaimed, his voice quivering just a bit, as though the sheer quality of the company was almost too much for him.

Everyone was gathered. Amanda and the fox terrier sat on a gold-hued picnic blanket with a checkered pattern. Albert sat down next to them, even though the rest of Everrock had taken other seats near Bengt's crooked wooden sculpture.

The band members wore sunglasses to avoid being recognised as public figures, but ended up resembling the mafia gang from Valö—or perhaps some other gang on the run from a low-budget film. Meanwhile, the white fox terrier growled softly but persistently at Albert, who, just as persistently, ignored it.

In front of Elaine's deckchair, the gourmand Bergling raised his champagne glass to the group, clearly relishing the moment.

"Zick-Zack saved me from certain death by drowning," he said, dramatically waving his glass. "And now, I must raise a toast to dear Captain Bengtsson and the two young ones. To your heroic efforts... I feared thirst, hunger, and... did I mention thirst? But you saved us and locked the villains away. A round of applause!"

Zacharias noted, disheartened, that Albert reached for Amanda's hand and clasped it firmly as Bergling mentioned their contribution.

"Uff," Maja said at the same moment, giving Bergling a disapproving look.

Zacharias placed the Camembert onto the plates with precision, while Bergling, undeterred, launched into what sounded like a drinking song to Elaine's recovery.

"Mind taking over here, Claes-Åke?" Zacharias asked quietly. "I think I'm off."

"Right," Claes-Åke replied, his tone as flat as a pancake.

He was still sulking after the row with Siw.

"Is it because of that chap in the leather jacket?" he added, rather bluntly.

"Well..." Zacharias said, looking a bit embarrassed. "I'm not really sure, to be honest. It's just..."

Maja, with a determined huff, set off with her rollator, only to immediately block Zacharias' path.

"My sugar-free potato buns?" she asked urgently, then added, "They're finally ready? About time!"

"I'm leaving," Zacharias repeated, trying to dodge her. "Ask Claes-Åke. He's in charge now."

"Ugh! Is he going, then? Just because those two are holding hands? Holding hands? That's nothing! Back in my day, we did far more than that. Let me tell you about a dance I went to... oh, let me think... yes, 1948. I was married at the time. But that didn't stop me from having a fling with my biggest admirer, Hjalmar. Holding hands? Pfft, we did much more than hold hands, we—"

"Maja, please," Claes-Åke said, cutting her off. "I've heard more than I need to!"

"Uff," Maja muttered. "Where did my sugar-free potato buns go?"

Just then, Zacharias noticed a silver-grey BMW swerving into the driveway.

Elaine's eyes widened in mild panic as she spotted the immaculately dressed politician, Caspar Richardsson. She gripped the armrest of the deckchair like she was about to make a hasty exit, perhaps even fold herself up with it. Caspar, meanwhile, ran a hand through his perfectly sculpted hair and presented her with a rather over-the-top bouquet of apricot-coloured lilies and white gerberas.

"I just popped by to wish you a speedy recovery," he said, all charm, "and to deliver these lovely flowers."

"I'm allergic to..." Elaine began, raising her hands in a futile attempt to ward him off. But Caspar, clearly un-deterred, dropped the bouquet straight into her lap without a second thought.

"You wouldn't believe the things I've been up to lately," he carried on, practically bursting with energy, while Elaine let out a massive sneeze. "Hectic doesn't even begin to cover it. But, you know, I'm this close to getting my foot in the door at the Riksdag after that little Hansson blunder. All in all, I still found time to pop over and check on you. I heard you were both unwell and a bit down in the dumps. Quite the bother, really. And it's a shame we won't be seeing each other as much in the future. With the parliament thing, I'll be hunting for an apartment in Stockholm, you see."

A hint of life returned to Elaine's tired face.

"See less of each other?"

"Yes, yes," Caspar said with a shrug, "but only a smidge, of course."

The scent of the lilies rose in a thick, heady cloud from the bouquet.

"Caspar," Amanda said, standing up to ease the situation. "Are you planning to stay for the picnic?"

In one swift motion, she relieved Elaine of the bouquet and concealed it behind her back.

"Well, you've certainly done a rather fine job here," Caspar said, surveying the scene with a smug smile, and both Amanda and Elaine braced themselves for the inevitable: "Of course I'll stay!"

"Caspar!"

Everyone turned to see Zacharias walking towards the landlord.

"Ah, about time you showed up! You wouldn't believe how hard I've been trying to get hold of you! Since you didn't lift a finger, I had to hire a builder to fix the leaking roof. Let me just find the invoice for the whole thing—it's around here somewhere."

Zacharias started searching through his jeans pockets.

At that very moment, Caspar chimed in:

"I was just about to say... Absolutely not. I can't stay a moment longer. Sorry, Elaine, we'll have to catch up another time. I've got a taxi waiting at home—got to run."

He gave Elaine's shoulder a quick pat as a goodbye, then was back in his shiny BMW in the blink of an eye.

"Hocus pocus," Zacharias declared, with barely any enthusiasm, showing his empty hands. "And that's apparently how you get rid of Caspar Richardsson."

"Thanks!" Elaine said, sinking back into the deckchair. "Now, if only the whole world would leave me alone."

Amanda gave Zacharias a grateful smile before sitting down next to Elaine on the grass.

"Are you really sure you don't want any company?" she asked, sounding concerned.

"Absolutely!" Elaine replied, her tone resolute.

"You know what I reckon…" Zacharias said, settling on Elaine's other side. "I think it's the total opposite, really."

Elaine gave him a doubtful look.

"You've been running away to the ends of the world trying to get some peace, but it's only left you completely exhausted," Zacharias added.

"Nobody's listening," Elaine grumbled from her deckchair.

Suddenly, it clicked for Amanda.

"Ah, I get it now!" she said, excitedly. "That's why you called it *The Megaphone*—because you needed to drown out everything else. It was your way of shouting for help."

"That's nonsense!" Elaine shot back.

"I don't think so," Zacharias replied, absent-mindedly pulling up a few blades of grass from the slightly overgrown lawn. "You thought you needed isolation and calm, but deep down, you just wanted to be heard. The thing is, you can't be heard in a vacuum. You need someone at the other end."

"A friend," Amanda said. "Or two."

"Are you saying that it's all a paradox?" Elaine said, looking thoughtful. She was starting to get used to the idea—she might even accept it.

"That's right!" Zacharias replied. "A paradox, like the birthday paradox."

"Sorry, what?" Albert cut in. He was still sitting on the picnic blanket, keeping a watchful eye on the growling Lou. "The birthday paradox?"

"Rounded to a 50.7 percent chance, the probability that in a group of 23 randomly selected people, two will share the same birthday," Zacharias said, sounding like a walking calculator.

"That's ridiculous," Albert argued. "There are 365 days in a year, come on."

"Exactly," Zacharias replied. "Hence the paradox."

Amanda tuned out the guys' talk and turned to Elaine with full attention, saying, "*I'm* listening."

A faint smile flickered across Elaine's face, spreading to her eyes like a spark of light.

In the background, Albert declared that he was about to investigate if the birthday paradox applied to the group present.

"Counting Pingo and Lou, obviously," he added.

Zacharias rolled his eyes.

"This is rather nice, actually," Elaine said, getting up from her deckchair. "Where do I find the Camembert and those ridiculously colourful cocktails everyone's been talking about?"